He Wasn't Sure Exactly When He Decided Gemma Westmoreland Was Destined To Be *His* Woman.

Probably the day she had arrived from college. The moment she got out of her car and raced over to her older brother's arms for a huge hug, Callum had felt as if he'd been hit over the head with a two-by-four—not once but twice. And when she'd turned that wonder-girl smile on him, he hadn't been the same since.

Gemma, the one with the fiery temper. The one a man would least be able to handle.

Yes, Callum was more than certain that Gemma was the woman for him.

Now he had the job of convincing her of that…in an unsuspecting way, since she was also a woman who thought a serious relationship was not for her. Gemma Westmoreland was determined never to let a man break her heart.

But Callum knew that was the one thing she didn't have to worry about.

Dear Reader,

When I first introduced Callum Austell in
Hot Westmoreland Nights, I knew he would be a
man to die for; a man who would know what he
wanted and would do whatever it took to get it. I
left no doubt in anyone's mind that Callum wanted
Gemma Westmoreland, and in this very special story
he plans to get what he wants.

But first he has to be gracious enough to give Gemma
what she wants, or what she thinks she wants. Gemma
and Callum's story is a special love affair that shows
the love and devotion of a man determined to win the
heart of the woman he loves, although that woman is
determined to keep her heart to herself.

I hope all of you enjoy reading Callum and Gemma's
story as much as I enjoyed writing it.

And I want to thank all of you who helped to make
Hot Westmoreland Nights a *New York Times* bestseller!

Happy reading!

Brenda Jackson

BRENDA JACKSON

WHAT A WESTMORELAND WANTS

Silhouette®

Desire

Published by Silhouette Books

America's Publisher of Contemporary Romance

To my husband, the love of my life and my best friend,
Gerald Jackson, Sr.

To everyone who enjoys reading about the Westmoreland family,
this one is for you!

Esteem her, and she will exalt you; embrace her,
and she will honor you.
—Proverbs 4:8

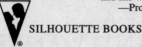

SILHOUETTE BOOKS

ISBN-13: 978-0-373-73048-3

WHAT A WESTMORELAND WANTS

Recycling programs
for this product may
not exist in your area.

BRENDA JACKSON

is a die "heart" romantic who married her childhood sweetheart and still proudly wears the "going steady" ring he gave her when she was fifteen. Because Brenda believes in the power of love, her stories always have happy endings. In her real-life love story, Brenda and her husband of thirty-eight years live in Jacksonville, Florida, and have two sons.

A *New York Times* bestselling author of more than seventy-five romance titles, Brenda is a recent retiree who now divides her time between family, writing and traveling with Gerald. You may write Brenda at P.O. Box 28267, Jacksonville, Florida 32226, by e-mail at WriterBJackson@aol.com or visit her Web site at www.brendajackson.net.

THE DENVER WESTMORELAND FAMILY TREE

Raphel and Gemma Westmoreland

Stern Westmoreland (Paula Bailey)

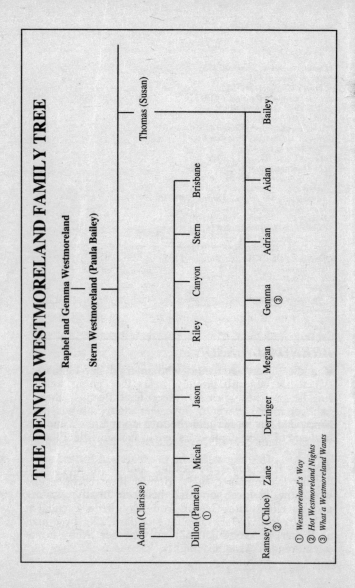

Thomas (Susan)

Adam (Clarisse)

Dillon (Pamela) ①

Micah — Jason — Riley — Canyon — Stern — Brisbane

Ramsey (Chloe) ② — Zane — Derringer — Megan — Gemma ③ — Adrian — Aidan — Bailey

① *Westmoreland's Way*
② *Hot Westmoreland Nights*
③ *What a Westmoreland Wants*

Prologue

Callum Austell sat in the chair with his legs stretched out in front of him as he stared at the man sitting behind the huge oak desk. He and Ramsey Westmoreland had become friends from the first, and now he had convinced Ramsey that he was the man who would give his sister Gemma the happiness she deserved.

But Callum knew there was one minor flaw in his plans. One that would come back to haunt him if Gemma Westmoreland ever discovered that the trip to Australia he would offer her would be orchestrated for the sole purpose of getting her off familiar turf so that she would finally come to realize just how much he cared for her.

"I hope you know what you're doing," Ramsey said, interrupting Callum's thoughts. "Gemma will give you hell when she finds out the truth."

"I'll tell her before then, but not before she falls in love with me," Callum replied.

Ramsey lifted a brow. "And if she doesn't?"

To any other woman Callum's intense pursuit might seem like a romantic move, but Ramsey was convinced his sister, who didn't have a romantic bone in her body, wouldn't see things that way.

Callum's expression was determined. "She will fall in love with me." And then the look in his eyes almost became one of desperation. "Damn, Ram, she has to. I knew the first moment I saw her that she was the one and only woman for me."

Ramsey took a deep breath. He wished he'd had the same thoughts the first time he set eyes on his wife, Chloe. Then he would not have encountered the problems he had. However, his first thoughts when he'd seen Chloe weren't the least bit honorable.

"You're my friend, Callum, but if you hurt my sister in any way, then you'll have one hell of an angry Westmoreland to deal with. Your intentions toward Gemma better be nothing but honorable."

Callum leaned forward in his chair. "I'm going to marry her."

"She has to agree to that first."

Callum stood. "She will. You just concentrate on becoming a father to the baby you and Chloe are expecting in a couple of months, and let me worry about Gemma."

One

Gem, I am sorry and I hope you can forgive me
one day.

—Niecee

Gemma Westmoreland lifted a brow after reading the
note that appeared on her computer after she'd booted
it up. Immediately, two questions sailed through her
mind. Where was Niecee when she should have been at
work over an hour ago and what was Niecee apologizing
for?

The hairs on the back of Gemma's neck began standing
up and she didn't like the feeling. She had hired Niecee
Carter six months ago when Designs by Gem began
picking up business, thanks to the huge contract she'd
gotten with the city of Denver to redecorate several of
its libraries. Then Gayla Mason had wanted her mansion

redone. And, last but not least, her sister-in-law, Chloe, hired Gemma for a makeover of the Denver branch of her successful magazine, *Simply Irresistible*.

Gemma had been badly in need of help and Niecee had possessed more clerical skills than the other candidates she'd interviewed. She had given the woman the job without fully checking out her references—something her oldest brother, Ramsey, had warned her against doing. But she hadn't listened. She'd figured that she and the bubbly Niecee would gel well. They had, but now, as Gemma quickly logged into her bank account, she couldn't help wondering if perhaps she should have taken Ramsey's advice.

Gemma had been eleven when Ramsey and her cousin Dillon had taken over the responsibility of raising their thirteen siblings after both sets of parents had been killed in a plane crash. During that time Ramsey had been her rock, the brother who'd been her protector. And now, it seemed, the brother she should have listened to when he'd handed out advice on how to run her business.

She pulled in a sharp breath when she glanced at the balance in her checking account. It was down by $20,000. Nervously, she clicked on the transaction button and saw that a $20,000 check had cleared her bank—a check that she hadn't written. Now she knew what Niecee's apology was all about.

Gemma dropped her face in her hands and felt the need to weep. But she refused to go there. She had to come up with a plan to replace that money. She was expecting invoices to come rolling in any day now from the fabric shops, arts and craft stores and her light fixtures suppliers, just to name a few. Clearly, she wouldn't have enough funds to pay all her debts. She needed to replace those funds.

She stood and began pacing the floor as anger consumed her. How could Niecee have done this to her? If she needed the money, all she had to do was ask. Although Gemma might not have been able to part with that much from her personal account, she could have borrowed the money from one of her brothers or cousins.

Gemma pulled in a deep frustrated breath. She had to file a police report. Her friendship and loyalty to Niecee ended the minute her former worker had stolen from her. She should have suspected something. Niecee hadn't been her usual bubbly self the last few days. Gemma figured it had to do with her trifling live-in boyfriend who barely worked. Had he put Niecee up to this? It didn't matter because Niecee should know right from wrong, and embezzling from your employer was wrong.

Sitting back down at her desk, Gemma reached for the phone and then pulled her hand back. Dang! If she called Sheriff Bart Harper—who had gone to school with both Ramsey and Dillon—and filed a report, there was no doubt in her mind that both Ram and Dillon would hear about it. Those were the last two people she wanted in her business. Especially since they'd tried talking her out of opening her interior design shop in the first place.

For the past year, things had worked out fairly well with her being just a one-woman show with her sisters, Megan and Bailey, helping out if needed. She had even pulled in her brothers, Zane and Derringer, on occasion, when heavy lifting had been involved. But when the big jobs began coming in, she had advertised in the newspapers and online for an administrative assistant.

She stood and began pacing again. Bailey was still taking classes at the university and wouldn't have that much money readily available, and Megan had mentioned just the other week that she was saving for a much-needed vacation. Megan was contemplating visiting their cousin, Delaney, who lived in the Middle East with her husband and two children, so there was no way she could hit her up for a loan.

Zane and Derringer were generous and because they were bachelors they might have that kind of ready dough. But they had recently pooled all their funds to buy into a horse-breeding and -training franchise, together with their cousin, Jason. She couldn't look in their direction now, due to that business venture. And all her other siblings and cousins were either in school or into their own businesses and investments.

So where was she going to get $20,000?

Gemma stood staring at the phone for a moment before it hit her that the thing was ringing. She quickly picked it up, hoping it was Niecee letting her know she was returning the money to her or, better yet, that the whole thing was a joke.

"Hello?"

"Hello, Gemma, this is Callum."

She wondered why the man who managed Ramsey's sheep farm would be calling her. "Yes, Callum?"

"I was wondering if I could meet with you sometime today to discuss a business proposition."

She lifted a brow. "A business proposition?"

"Yes."

The first thought that crossed her mind was that engaging in a business meeting was the last thing she was in the mood for today. But then she quickly realized that she couldn't let what Niecee did keep her from handling things with her company. She still had a business to run.

"When would you like to meet, Callum?"

"How about today for lunch."

"Lunch?"

"Yes, at McKay's."

She wondered if he knew that McKay's was her favorite lunch spot. "Okay, that'll work. I'll see you there at noon," she said.

"Great. See you then."

Gemma held the phone in her hand, thinking how much she enjoyed listening to Callum's deep Australian accent. He always sounded so ultrasexy. But then he was definitely a sexy man. That was something she tried not to notice too much, mainly because he was a close friend of Ramsey's. Also, according to Jackie Barnes, a nurse who worked at the hospital with Megan and who'd had a bad case of the hots for Callum when he first arrived in Denver, Callum had a girl waiting for him back in Australia and it was a very serious relationship.

But what if he no longer had that girl waiting for him back in Australia? What if he was as available as he was hot? What if she could forget that he was her oldest brother's close friend? What if…

Dismissing all such thoughts with a wave of her hand, she sat back down at her computer to figure out a way to rob Peter to pay Paul.

* * *

Callum Austell leaned back in his chair as he glanced around the restaurant. The first time he'd eaten here had been with Ramsey when he first came to Denver. He liked it then and now this would be the place where he would put into motion a plan some would think was way past due being executed. He would have to admit they were probably right.

He wasn't sure exactly when he decided that Gemma Westmoreland was destined to be *his* woman. Probably the day he had helped Ramsey build that barn and Gemma had arrived from college right after graduation. The moment she got out of her car and raced over to her older brother's arms for a huge hug. Callum had felt like he'd gotten hit over the head with a two-by-four, not once but twice. And when Ramsey had introduced them and she'd turned that wondergirl smile on him, he hadn't been the same since. His father and his two older brothers had warned him that it would be that way when he found the woman destined to be his, but he hadn't believed them.

That had been almost three years ago and she'd been just twenty-two years old. So he'd waited patiently for her to get older and had watched over her from afar. And each passing day she'd staked a deeper claim to his heart. Knowing how protective Ramsey was of his siblings, especially his three sisters, Callum had finally gotten up the nerve to confront Ramsey and tell him how he felt about Gemma.

At first Ramsey hadn't liked the idea of his best friend lusting after one of his sisters. But then Callum had convinced Ramsey it was more than lust and that he knew in his heart that Gemma was "the one" for him.

For six months, Ramsey had lived with Callum's family back in Australia on the Austell sheep ranch to learn everything he could so he could start his own operations in Denver. He had hung around Callum's parents and brothers enough to know how dedicated the Austell men were once they fell in love.

His father had given up on falling in love and was on his way back to Australia from a business meeting in the United States to marry an Australian woman when he'd met Callum's mother. She was one of the flight attendants on the plane.

Somehow the already engaged Todd Austell had convinced the Detroit-born Le'Claire Richards that breaking off with his fiancée and marrying her instead was the right thing to do. Evidently it was. Thirty-seven years later the two were still married, remained very much in love and had three sons and a daughter to show for it. Callum was the youngest of the four and the only one who was still single.

His thoughts shifted back to Gemma. Ramsey claimed that of his three sisters, Gemma was the one with the fiery temper. The one a man would least be able to handle. He'd suggested that Callum pray long and hard about making the right decision.

In the end, Callum had convinced Ramsey that he had made the right decision and that a hard-to-handle woman with a fiery temper was the kind he liked. He was more than certain that Gemma was the woman for him.

Now he had to convince Gemma… He'd have to be

stealthy about his pursuit. He knew Gemma had no intention of engaging in a serious relationship after she had witnessed how two of her brothers, and several of her womanizing cousins, had operated with women over the years, breaking hearts in their wake. According to Ramsey, Gemma Westmoreland was determined never to let a man break her heart.

Callum straightened up in his seat when he saw Gemma enter the restaurant. Immediately, the same feeling suffused his heart that always settled there whenever he saw her. He loved the woman. He no longer tried to rationalize why. It really didn't matter at this point.

As she walked toward him, he stood. She was probably 5'8", but just the right height for his 6'3" frame. And he'd always thought she had a rather nice figure. Her dark brown, shoulder-length hair was pulled back in a ponytail. He thought she had dazzling tawny-brown eyes, which were almost covered by her bangs.

Callum had worked hard not to give his feelings away. Because he'd always been on his best behavior around her, he knew she didn't have a clue. It hadn't been easy keeping her in the dark. She saw him as nothing more than her brother's best friend from Australia. The Aussie who didn't have a lot to say and was basically a loner.

He studied her expression as she got closer. She seemed anxious, as if she had a lot on her mind.

"Callum," she said and smiled.

"Gemma. Thanks for agreeing to see me," he said as he took her oustretched hand.

"No problem," she said, sitting down once he released her hand. "You said something about meeting to discuss a business proposition."

"Yes, but first how about us grabbing something to eat. I'm starving."

"Sure."

As if on cue, a waitress strolled over with menus and placed glasses of water in front of them. "I hope this place is acceptable," Callum said, moments later after taking a sip of his water.

"Trust me, it is," Gemma said smiling. "It's one of my favorites. The salads here are fabulous."

He chuckled. "Are they?"

"Yes."

"That might very well be, but I'm not a salad man. I prefer something a lot heavier. Like a steak and the French fries I hear this place is famous for."

"No wonder you and Ramsey get along. Now that he's married to Chloe, I'll bet he's in hog heaven with all those different meals she likes to prepare."

"I'm sure he is. It's hard to believe he's married," Callum said.

"Yes, four months tomorrow and I don't recall my brother ever being happier."

"And his men are happy, too, now that Nellie's been replaced as cook," he said. "She never could get her act together and it worked out well for everyone when she decided to move closer to her sister when her marriage fell apart."

Gemma nodded. "I hear the new cook is working out wonderfully, although most of the guys still prefer Chloe's cooking. But she is happy just being Ramsey's wife and a mother-in-waiting. She doesn't have long now and I'm excited about becoming an aunt.

"Are you an uncle yet?"

It was his turn to smile. "Yes. My two older brothers and one sister are married with a child each. I'm used to being around kids. And I also have a goddaughter who will be celebrating her first birthday soon."

At that moment the waitress returned. Callum resented the interruption.

Gemma appreciated the interruption. Although she had been around Callum plenty of times, she'd never noticed just how powerfully built he was. Her brothers and male cousins were all big men, but Callum was so much more manly.

And she had to listen carefully to what he said and stop paying so much attention to how he said it. His thick Australian accent did things to her. It sent a warm, sensual caress across her skin every time he opened his mouth to speak. Then there were his looks, which made her understand perfectly why Jackie Barnes and quite a number of other women had gone bonkers over him. In addition to being tall, with a raw, masculine build, he had thick chestnut-brown hair that fell to his shoulders. Most days he wore it pulled back into a ponytail. He'd made today an exception and it cascaded around his shoulders.

Gemma had once overheard him mention to her sister, Megan, that his full lips and dark hair came from his African-American mother and his green eyes and his square jaw from his father. She'd also heard him say that his parents had met on an airplane. His mother had been a flight attendant on his father's flight from the United States back to Australia. He'd told Megan it had been love at first sight, which made her wonder if he believed in such nonsense. She knew there was no such thing.

"So what do you think of Dillon and Pamela's news?"

Callum's question cut into her thoughts and she glanced up to meet his green eyes. She swallowed. Was there a hint of blue in their depths. And then there was his dimpled smile that took her breath away.

"I think it's wonderful," she said, suddenly feeling the need to take a sip of cold water. "There haven't been babies in our family in a long time. With Chloe expecting and now Pamela, that's two babies to spoil and I can't wait."

"You like children?"

She chuckled. "Yes, unfortunately, I'm one of those people who take to the precious darlings a little too much. That's why my friends call on me more often than not to babysit for them."

"You could always marry and have your own."

She made a face. "Thanks, but no thanks. At least no time soon, if ever. I'm sure you've heard the family joke about me never wanting to get serious about a man. Well, it's not a joke—it's the truth."

"Because of what you witnessed with your brothers while growing up?"

So he *had* heard. Any one of her brothers could have mentioned it, especially because she denounced their behavior every chance she got. "I guess you can say I saw and heard too much. My brothers and cousins had a reputation for fast cars and fast women. They thought nothing about breaking hearts. Ramsey usually had a steady girl, but Zane and Derringer were two of the worst when it came to playing women. As far as I'm concerned, they still are." Unfortunately, she'd overheard one of Zane's phone calls that very morning when she had stopped by to borrow some milk.

"I can clearly recall the times when Megan and I, and sometimes even Bailey, who was still young enough to be playing with her dolls, would be the ones to get the phone calls from love-stricken girls in tears after being mercilessly dumped by one of my brothers or cousins."

And they were females determined to share their teary-eyed, heart-wrenching stories with anyone willing to listen. Megan and Bailey would get them off the phone really quickly, but Gemma had been the bleeding heart. She would ease into a chair and take the time to listen to their sob stories, absorbing every heartbreaking detail like a sponge. Even to the point at which she would end up crying a river of tears right along with them.

She'd decided by the time she had begun dating that no man alive would make her one of those weeping women. And then there was this inner fear she'd shared with no one, the fear of falling in love and having the person abandon her one day…the way she felt whenever she thought about her parents. She knew she had no logical reason for feeling abandoned by them because she was certain if they'd had a choice they would have survived that plane crash. But still, as illogical as it might be, the fear was there for her and it was real. She was convinced there was no man worth a single Gemma Westmoreland tear or her fears, and intended to make sure she never shed one by never giving her heart to anyone. She would be celebrating her twenty-fifth birthday in a few months and so far she'd managed to keep both her heart and her virginity intact.

"And because of that you don't ever plan to get seriously involved with a man?"

She drew in a deep breath. She and her sisters had had this conversation many times and she was wondering why she was sitting here having it with Callum now. Why was he interested? It dawned on her that he probably wasn't; he was just asking to fill the time. "As far as I'm concerned that's a good enough reason. Those girls were in love with my brothers and cousins and assumed they loved them back. Just look what that wrong assumption did to them."

Callum took a sip of his water, deciding not to respond by saying that as far as he was concerned her brothers' behavior was normal for most men, and in some cases women. Granted, he hadn't been around Zane and Derringer while they had been in their teens and could just imagine some of the things they had gotten in to. Now, as grown men, he knew they enjoyed women, but then most hot-blooded men did. And just because a man might be considered a "player" somewhat before finally settling down with one woman—the one he chose to spend the rest of his life with—that didn't necessarily mean he was a man who totally disrespected women. In fairness to Zane and Derringer, they treated women with respect.

He wondered what she would think if she knew how his behavior had been before he'd met her. He hadn't considered himself a womanizer, although he'd dated a slew of woman. He merely thought of himself as a man who enjoyed life and wanted to have a good time with the opposite sex while waiting for the girl destined to share his life to come along. Once she had, he'd had no trouble bringing his fun-loving, footloose and fancy-free bachelor lifestyle to an end. Eventually, the same thing would happen to her brothers and cousins.

No wonder her brothers thought she was a lost cause, but he refused to accept that. He was determined to show her how things could be if she were to fall in love with a man committed to making her happy.

In a way, he felt he knew Gemma. He believed that beneath her rough and tough "I'll never fall in love" exterior was the heart of a woman who not only loved children but loved life in general. He also believed that she was a passionate woman. And that she was unknowingly reserving that passion for the one man capable of tapping into it. The same man destined to spend the rest of his life with her. Him.

The waitress delivered their food, and they engaged in chitchat while they ate their meal.

After they had finished eating and the waitress removed their plates, Gemma leaned back in her chair and smiled at Callum. "Lunch was wonderful. Now, about that business proposition?"

He chuckled, reached over and picked up the folder he had placed on an empty chair. He handed it to her. "This is information on the home I purchased last year. I would love you to decorate it for me."

Callum saw how her eyes lit up. She loved her work and it showed in her face. She opened the folder and carefully studied every feature, every detail of the house. He knew exactly what he was doing. He was giving her

9,200 feet of house to do with as she pleased. It was an interior designer's dream.

She lifted her gaze with a look of awe on her face. "This place is beautiful. And it's huge. I didn't know you had purchased a house."

"Yes, but it's still empty and I want to turn it into a home. I like what you did with Ramsey's place and thought you would be the ideal person for the job. I'm aware that because of the size of the house it will take up a lot of your time. I'm willing to pay you well. As you can see I haven't picked out any furniture or anything. I wouldn't know where to begin."

Now that much was true, Callum thought. What he didn't tell her was that other designers had volunteered to decorate his new house, but he had bought it with her in mind.

She glanced back down at the papers in front of her. "Umm, eight bedrooms, six bathrooms, a huge kitchen, living room, dining room, family room, theater, recreation room and sauna. That's quite a lot of space for a single man."

He laughed. "Yeah, but I don't plan on staying single forever."

Gemma nodded, thinking that evidently Callum had decided to settle down and send for that girl back home. She glanced down at the papers again. She would love taking on this project, and he was right in thinking it would take up a lot of her time. But then she definitely needed the money.

"So, what do you think, Gemma?"

She glanced back up at him and smiled. "I think you just hired yourself an interior designer."

The smile that touched his face sent a tingling sensation flowing through her stomach. "I can't wait to see it."

"No problem. When can you get away?"

She pulled out her cell phone to check her calendar and her schedule for this week. Once she saw the place and gave him an official estimate, she could ask for a deposit, which would make up some of what Niecee had taken from her. "What about tomorrow around one?"

"That might be a bit of a problem."

"Oh." She figured he would probably be tied up at Ram's ranch doing something at that time, so without looking up she advanced her calendar another day. "What about Wednesday around noon."

He chuckled. "Twelve noon on Monday would be the earliest availability for me."

She nodded when she saw that time was free for her, although she wished she could see it sooner. "Monday at noon will be fine."

"Great, I'll make the necessary flight arrangements."

She put her phone back into her purse and glanced over at him. "Excuse me?"

"I said that I will make the necessary flight arrangements if we want to see the house Monday at noon. That means we'll need to fly out no later than Thursday morning."

Gemma frowned. "Thursday morning? What are you talking about? Just where is this house located?"

Callum leaned back in his chair and gave her one kilowatt smile. "Sydney, Australia."

Two

Gemma didn't have to look in the mirror to know there was a shocked look on her face. And her throat felt tight, as if sound would barely pass through it if she tried to speak. To prove the point, she tried to utter a word and couldn't. So she just sat there and stared across the table at Callum like he had lost his ever-loving mind.

"Now that that's all settled, let's order some dessert," Callum said, picking up the menu.

She reached out, touched his hand and shook her head. "What's the matter?" he asked. "You don't want dessert?"

She drew in a deep breath, made an attempt to speak once more and was glad when sound came out. But to be absolutely sure he understood, she held up her hands in the shape of a T. "Time-out."

He lifted an eyebrow. "Time-out?"

She nodded. "Yes, time-out. You lost me between the flight on Thursday and Sydney, Australia. Are you saying this house that you want me to decorate is in Sydney, Australia?"

"Of course. Where else would it be?"

She fought hard not to glare at him; after all, he was a potential client. "I thought possibly in the Denver area," she said in what she hoped was a neutral tone.

"Why would you think that?"

She couldn't hold back her glare any longer. "Well, you've been in this country for almost three years now."

"Yes, but I've never said or insinuated to anyone that I wouldn't return home. I was here helping Ramsey out and now that he has the hang of things, I'm no longer needed. Now I can get back home and—"

"Get married," Gemma supplied.

He chuckled. "As I said earlier, I don't plan on staying single forever."

"And when do you plan on marrying her?"

"Her who?"

Gemma wondered why some men suddenly went daft when their girlfriends were mentioned. "The woman waiting for you back in Australia."

"Umm, I didn't know there was such a creature."

Gemma stared at him in disbelief. "Are you saying you don't have a fiancée or a sweetheart back in Australia?"

He smiled. "That's exactly what I'm saying. Where did you hear something like that?"

Normally Gemma wouldn't divulge her sources, but typically, Jackie knew what she was talking about, and that wouldn't be anything the woman would have made up. "Jackie Barnes. And everyone figured she got the information from you."

Callum shook his head. "She didn't get that from me, but I have an idea where it came from. Your brother, Zane. I complained about Jackie making a nuisance of herself and he figured the best way to get rid of a woman like Jackie was just to let her believe I was already taken."

"Oh." She could see Zane doing something like that. If for no other reason than to shift Jackie's interest from Callum to him. Her brother was a womanizer to the nth degree. And Derringer wasn't any better. It was a blessing that the twins, Adrian and Aidan, were away at college, where the only thing on their minds was making the grade. "I assume Zane's plan worked."

"It did."

"In that case you were lucky," Gemma decided to say. "Some women would not have cared that you were spoken for. They would have taken it as a challenge to swing your interest their way."

Callum couldn't help but think of just where his interest had been for the past three years and knew no one could have succeeded in doing that. The woman sitting across the table was the one he intended to marry.

"And you actually assumed I have someone of interest back home?"

She shrugged. "Hey, that's what we all heard and I had no reason to assume differently. As far as I knew, you weren't dating anyone and whenever we had events you always came alone."

And tried hanging around you every chance I got,
he thought.

"You were almost as much of a loner as Ramsey,"
Gemma added. "If your goal was to keep the women
away, then it evidently worked for you."

He took a sip of his drink, wondering if the reason
she had yet to pick up on his interest in her was because
she figured he was already taken.

"Callum, about this trip to Australia?"

He knew where she was about to take the discussion
and was prepared with a spiel to reel her in. "What
about it? If you're having second thoughts, I understand.
No sweat. I've already contacted a backup in case you
couldn't do it. Jeri Holliday at Jeri's Fashion Designs
has indicated she would love the job and will have her
bags packed for Australia before I can blink an eye."

Over my dead body, Gemma thought as she sat up
straight in her chair. Jeri Holliday had been trying to
steal clients from her for years.

"I think she liked the fact that I'm offering $50,000,
and half of that upfront."

His words froze her thoughts. "Come again?"

He smiled. "I said, considering that I'm asking the
decorator to give up at least six weeks, I'm offering
$50,000, just as a starting price."

Gemma could only stare at him once again in
disbelief. She leaned closer to the table and spoke in
a hushed tone, as if anyone sitting in close range could
overhear their top-secret conversation. "Are you saying
that you're paying $25,000 on acceptance of the job and
the other half on completion; and that $50,000 does not
include any of the materials? That's just for labor?"

"Yes, that's what I'm saying."

Gemma began nibbling on her bottom lip. The $25,000 would definitely boost her bank account, replacing what Niecee had stolen. And then to think there would be another $25,000 waiting when she completed everything. However, as good as it sounded there were a few possible conflicts.

"What do you see as the time line for this project, Callum?" she decided to ask him.

He shrugged wide shoulders. "I'll tell you the same thing I told Jeri. I think it will take a month to six weeks to take down all the measurements and get things ordered. I'd also like that person there to coordinate the selection of all the furniture. However, there's no rush on that."

Gemma began nibbling on her lips again. "The reason I asked is because there are two babies who will be born within a few months of each other and I'd like to be here for both births. If I can't make it back at the time of delivery then at least within a few days."

"No problem. In fact, I'll spring for the flight."

Gemma couldn't help but wonder why he was being so generous and decided to ask him.

"I've always believed in being fair when it came to those who worked for me," he said.

"In any case, I'm going to need to return myself to help out because Ramsey will be busy with Chloe and the baby," he continued. "I don't want him to worry about the ranch during that time, so I've already promised him that I would return. And although Dillon probably won't need me to do anything, he and Pamela are like family and I want to be here for their baby's arrival, too."

Gemma felt relieved. But still—Australia? That was such a long way from home. And for a month, possibly six weeks. The only other time she'd been away from home for so long was when she left for college in Nebraska. Now she was considering trekking off to another country. Heck, it was another continent.

She was suddenly filled with an anticipation she'd never felt before. She'd never been a traveler, but if she took Callum's job offer, she would get to see a part of the world she'd only read about. That was exciting.

"So are you still interested or do you want me to go with Jeri Holliday?"

She didn't hesitate. "I don't have a problem traveling to Australia and will be ready to fly out on Thursday. I just need to get my business in order. I'll be gone for a while and I'll need to let my family know."

It then occurred to her that her family might not like the idea of her going so far away. Ramsey had a tendency to be overprotective. But he had his hands full with Chloe expecting their baby at the end of November. He would be too busy to try to micromanage her life…thank goodness.

"Terrific. I'll make flight arrangements and will let you know when I have everything in order."

"All right."

Callum lifted up his soda glass in a toast. "Here's to adventures awaiting you in the outback."

Gemma chuckled as she lifted her glass in a toast, as well. "Yes, here's to adventures in the outback."

A few hours later back at her house, despite her outer calm, Gemma was trying to keep things together on the inside while she explained everything to her sisters, Megan and Bailey, as they sat together at the kitchen table. Megan was the oldest at twenty-six and Bailey was twenty-two.

"And why didn't you file a police report? Twenty thousand dollars isn't a little bit of money, Gem," an angry Megan wanted to know.

Gemma drew in a deep breath. "I'm working with the bank's security team in trying to recover the funds. The main reason I didn't get Sheriff Harper involved is because he's close friends with both Dillon and Ramsey. He'll probably get a report of the incident from the bank, eventually, but I think he'd be more inclined to keep his mouth shut about it. It would appear more of an official matter then."

"Oh."

From the look on her sisters' faces and their simultaneous responses, she knew they had forgotten that one important piece of information. There wasn't too much a Westmoreland did in these parts that Dillon and Ramsey didn't know about. Sheriff Harper, who had gone to high school with Dillon and Ramsey, made sure of that.

"And I didn't want to hear, 'I told you so' from those two. Neither of them wanted me to start my own business when I did. So there was no way I was going to tell them what Niecee had done. Hiring her was my mistake and I'll have to deal with it in my own way."

"But will you make sure she doesn't get away with her crime? I'd hate for her to steal from some other unsuspecting soul."

"Yes, I'm going to make sure she doesn't do this

again. And to think that I trusted her," Gemma said with a nod.

"You're too trusting," Megan said. "I've always warned you about that."

And she had, Gemma thought. So had her older brothers. "So what do you think about me going to Australia?" She needed to change the subject.

Megan smiled. "Personally, I think it's cool and wish I could go with you, but I'm saving my time off at the hospital for that trip to visit Delaney in Tehran."

"I think that's cool, as well," Bailey said. "I'm still reeling over the fact that there's no woman waiting for Callum back in Sydney. If that's true, then why isn't he dating? I don't ever recall him having a girlfriend while he's been here in the States. He's nothing like Zane and Derringer."

"And he's such a cutie-pie," Megan added.

Gemma couldn't help smiling as she recalled how sexy he looked sitting across from her at lunch. "He'd already mentioned the job to Jeri Holliday, but it was contingent on whether or not I would accept his offer."

"And I'm sure she was ready to grab it," Bailey said with a frown.

"Of course she was. I wish the two of you could see the size of his house. I can't believe he'd buy such a place as a single man. Now that I've made up my mind about going to Australia, I need to let Ramsey know."

Gemma inhaled sharply at the thought of doing that, but knew it needed to be done. However, under no circumstances did Ramsey need to know that Niecee had embezzled $20,000 from her. She would let the bank's security team handle things.

"You don't have any appointments or projects scheduled for the next six weeks?" Megan asked as they helped her pack.

"No. This job offer came at a good time. I had thought about taking a well-deserved vacation anyway, but now it's back to work for me. I'll take some time off during the holidays."

"If Callum bought a house in Australia, does that mean he's moving back home?"

Gemma glanced over at Bailey. That thought hadn't occurred to her. "I guess so."

"What a bummer. I've gotten used to seeing him," Bailey said with a pout. "I'd begun thinking of him as another big brother."

Gemma drew in a deep breath. For some reason she'd never thought of him as another big brother.

She'd never felt the need to become as friendly with him as Megan and Bailey had, but she never knew why she'd been standoffish with him. She'd only accepted that that was the way things were. Why now, all of a sudden, did the thought of him returning to Australia to live and her not seeing him ever again seem like such a big deal?

The very thought made her uneasy.

Three

"Are you okay, Gemma?"

Gemma turned her head to glance over at Callum.
What had the pilot just said? They were now cruising
at an altitude of 36,000 feet. Was Callum inquiring as
to how she felt because she'd suddenly turned green?

Now was not the time to tell him that she had an
aversion to flying. Although she'd flown before, that
didn't mean she liked it. In fact, she didn't. She'd told
herself while packing that she could handle the eighteen
hours it would take to get to Australia. Now she was
having some pretty serious doubts about that.

"Gemma?"

She drew in a deep breath. "Yes, I'm fine."

"You sure?"

No, she wasn't sure, but he would be the last person
to know. "Yes."

She turned her head to look out the window and wondered if asking for a window seat had been a wise choice. All she could see were clouds and Callum's reflection. He smelled good, and she couldn't help wondering what cologne he was wearing. And he looked good, too. He had arrived to pick her up wearing a pair of jeans, a blue chambray shirt and Western boots. She'd seen him in similar outfits plenty of times, but for some odd reason he seemed different to her today.

"The attendant is about to serve snacks. Are you hungry?"

She turned and met his eyes. They were a beautiful green and she could swear that a strange expression shone in their dark depths. "No, I ate a good breakfast this morning with Ramsey and Chloe."

He lifted a brow. "You got up at five this morning to do that?"

She smiled. "Yes. All I had to do was set the alarm. I figured if I got up early, then by the time this plane leveled off in the sky I would be ready to take a nap."

He chuckled. "Does flying bother you?"

"Let's just say it's not one of my favorite things to do," she answered. "There're other things I prefer doing more. Like getting a root canal or something else equally as enjoyable."

He threw his head back and laughed, and she liked the sound of it. She'd known him for almost three years and this was the first time she recalled hearing him laugh. He'd always seemed so serious, just like Ramsey. At least that was how Ramsey used to be. She would be one of the first to say that marriage had changed her brother for the better.

"And then," she added in a soft, thoughtful tone. "My parents were killed in a plane crash and I can't help but think of that whenever I'm in the air." She paused a moment. "There was a time after their deaths that I swore I'd never get on a plane," she said quietly.

Callum did something at that moment she hadn't expected. He reached out and took her hand in his. His was warm and large and completely covered hers. "How did you overcome that fear?"

She shifted her gaze away from their joined hands to his face and sighed deeply. "I refused to live my life in fear of the unknown. So one day I went to Ramsey and told him I was ready to take my first plane ride. He was working with Dillon at Blue Ridge Land Management at the time and made arrangements to take me on his next business trip. I was fourteen."

A bright smile touched her lips. "He signed me out of school for a few days and I flew with him to New Mexico. My first encounter with turbulence almost sent me through the roof. But he talked me through it. He even made me write an essay on my airplane experience."

The flight attendant came around serving drinks and snacks, but Gemma declined everything. Callum took a pack of peanuts and ordered a beer. Gemma had asked for a pillow earlier and adjusted it against her neck as she reclined comfortably in her seat. She had to admit that the first-class seats on this international flight were spacious. And Callum had booked a double-seat row for just the two of them.

Gemma noticed that the attendant had given Callum one or two smiles more than was necessary. The attendant's obvious interest in her passenger made Gemma think of something. "Is it true that your parents met on a flight to Australia?"

He inclined his head to look at her. "Yes, that's true. Dad was actually engaged to someone else at the time and was returning home to Australia to help plan his wedding."

"And he fell for someone else when he was already engaged?"

Callum heard the shock in her voice. Considering what she thought about men deliberately breaking women's hearts, he decided to explain. "From what I was told, he had asked this woman to marry him and it was to be a marriage of convenience."

She lifted a brow. "A marriage of convenience for whom?"

"The both of them. She wanted a rich husband and he wanted a wife to start a family. They saw it as the perfect union."

Gemma nodded. "So love had nothing to do with it?"

"No. He didn't think such a thing could exist for him until he saw my mother. He was hit between the eyes with a ton of bricks." Callum chuckled. "Those are his words, not mine."

"And what happened to the other woman? The one he'd been engaged to at the time?"

He could hear pity in her voice. "Not sure. But I know what didn't happen to her."

Gemma lifted a curious brow. "What?"

A smile touched his lips. "She didn't get the wedding she planned."

"And you find that amusing?"

"Actually, yes, because it was discovered months later that she was pregnant with another man's child."

Gemma gasped sharply and leaned her head closer to Callum's. "Are you serious?"

"Very much so."

"The same thing almost happened to Ramsey, but Danielle stopped the wedding," Gemma said.

"So I heard."

"And I liked her."

"I heard that, too. I understand that your entire family did. But then that goes to show."

She looked over at him. "What?"

"Men aren't the only ones who can be heart-breakers."

Surprise swept across her face at his remark. Gemma leaned back against her seat and released her breath in a slow sigh. "I never said they were."

"You didn't?" he asked smiling.

"No, of course not."

Callum decided not to argue with her about it. Instead, he just smiled. "It's time for that nap. You're beginning to sound a bit grouchy."

To Callum's surprise, she took one, which gave him the opportunity to watch her while she slept. As he gazed at her, he experienced the same intense desire that he'd always felt whenever he was close to her. At the moment, he was close, but not close enough. He couldn't help but study her features and thought her moments of peaceful bliss had transformed her already beautiful face into one that was even more striking.

He would be the first to admit that she no longer looked like the young girl he'd seen that first day. In three years, her features had changed from that of a girl to a woman and it all started with the shape of her mouth, which was nothing short of sensuous. How could lips be that full and inviting, he wondered, as his gaze moved from one corner of her mouth to the other.

Callum's gaze drifted upward from her mouth to her closed eyes and the long lashes covering them. His gaze then moved to her cheekbones and he was tempted to take the back of his hand and caress them, or better yet, trace their beautiful curves with the tip of his tongue, branding her as his. And she *was* his, whether she knew it or not, whether she accepted it or not. She belonged to him.

He then noticed how even her breathing was, and how every breath drew his attention to the swell of her breasts that were alluringly hidden inside a light blue blouse. He'd always found her sexy, too sexy, and it had been hard not to want her, so he hadn't even bothered fighting the temptation. He had lusted after her from afar, which was something he couldn't help, since he hadn't touched another woman in almost three years. Once her place in his life had become crystal clear, his body had gone into a disciplined mode, knowing she would be the one and only woman he would make love to for the rest of his life. Now, the thought of that made his body go hard. He breathed in her scent, he closed the book he had been reading and adjusted his pillow. He closed his eyes and allowed his fantasies of her to do what they always did, take over his mind and do in his dreams what he couldn't yet do in reality.

* * *

Gemma slowly opened her eyes at the same moment she shifted in her seat. She glanced over at Callum and saw that he had fallen asleep. His head was tilted close to hers.

She would have to admit that at first his close proximity had bothered her because she assumed they would have to make a lot of unnecessary conversation during the flight. She wasn't very good at small talk or flirting. She'd dated before, but rarely, because most men had a tendency to bore her. She'd discovered that most liked talking about themselves, tooting their own horn and figured they were God's gift to women.

She pushed all thoughts of other men aside and decided to concentrate on this one. He was sitting so close that she could inhale his masculine scent. She had enough brothers and male cousins to know that just as no two women carried the same scent, the same held true for men. Each person's fragrance was unique and the one floating through her nostrils now was making funny feelings flutter around in her stomach.

Gemma found it odd that nothing like this had ever happened to her before, but then she couldn't recall Callum ever being this close to her. Usually they were surrounded by other family members. Granted, they weren't exactly alone now, but, still, there was a sense of intimacy with him sitting beside her. She could just make out the soft sounds of his even breathing.

She had been ready to go when he had arrived at her place. When she opened the door and he had walked in, her breath had gotten caught in her throat. She'd seen him in jeans more times than not, but there was something about the pair he was wearing now that had caused her to do a double take. When he'd leaned down to pick up her luggage, his masculine thighs flexed beneath starched denim. Then there were those muscled arms beneath the Western shirt. Her gaze had lingered longer than it should have on his body. She had followed him out the door while getting an eyeful of his make-you-want-to-drool tush.

She studied him now, fascinated by just what a good-looking man he was and how he'd managed to keep women at bay for so long. A part of her knew it hadn't just been the story Zane had fabricated about a woman waiting for him back in Australia. That tale might have kept some women like Jackie away, but it would not have done anything to hold back the bolder ones. It was primarily the way he'd carried himself. Just like Ramsey. In his pre-Chloe days, most women would have thought twice before approaching her brother. He radiated that kind of "I'm not in the mood" aura whenever it suited him.

But for some reason, she'd never considered Callum as unapproachable as Ramsey. Whenever they had exchanged words, he'd been friendly enough with her. A part of her was curious about why if he wasn't already taken; he'd held himself back from engaging in a serious relationship with a woman. Perhaps he wanted a wife who was from his homeland. That wouldn't be surprising, although it was ironic that his mother was American.

"Oh." The word slipped through her lips in a frantic tone when the plane shook from the force of strong turbulence. She quickly caught her breath.

"You okay?"

She glanced over at Callum. He was awake. "Yes. I hadn't expected that just then. Sorry if I woke you up."

"No problem," he said, straightening up in his seat. "We've been in the air about four hours now, so we were bound to hit an air pocket sooner or later."

She swallowed when the airplane hit a smaller, less forceful pocket of turbulence. "And they don't bother you?"

"Not as much as they used to. When I was younger, my siblings and I would fly with Mom back to the States to visit our grandparents. I used to consider turbulence as exciting as a roller-coaster ride. I thought it was fun."

Gemma rolled her eyes. "There's nothing fun about the feel of an airplane shaking all over the place like it's about to come apart."

He released a soft chuckle. "You're safe, but let me check your seat belt to be sure."

Before she could pull in her next breath, he reached out to her waist and touched her seat belt. She felt his fingers brush against her stomach in the process. At that precise moment, sensations rushed all through her belly and right up her arms.

She glanced over at Callum and found her gaze ensnared by the deep green of his eyes and those sensations intensified. She knew at that moment that something was happening between them, and whatever it was, she wasn't quite prepared for it.

She'd heard about sexual awareness, but why would it affect her now, and why with someone who was almost a total stranger to her? It wasn't as if this was the first time she and Callum had been around each other. But then…as she'd acknowledged to herself earlier, this was the first time they had been alone to this degree. She wondered if her new feelings were one-sided, or if he'd felt it, as well.

"You're belted tight," he said, and to her his voice seemed a bit huskier…or perhaps she was just imagining things.

"Thanks for checking."

"No problem."

Since they were both wide awake now, Gemma decided it was probably a good idea to engage in conversation. That would be safer than just sitting here and letting all kinds of crazy thoughts race through her mind, like what would happen if she were to check on his seat belt as he'd checked on hers. She felt heat infuse her face and her heart rate suddenly shot up.

Then her anxiety level moved up a notch when she thought his gaze lingered on her lips a little longer than necessary. Had that really been the case? "Tell me about Australia," she said quickly.

Evidently talking about his homeland was something he enjoyed doing if the smile tilting his lips was anything to go by. And they were a gorgeous pair. She'd noticed them before, but this was the first time she'd given those lips more than a passing thought.

Why all of a sudden was there something so compelling about Callum? Why did the thought of his lips, eyes and other facial features, as well as his hands and fingers, suddenly make her feel hot?

"You're going to love Australia," he said, speaking in

that deep accent she loved hearing. "Especially Sydney. There's no place in the world quite like it."

She lifted a brow and folded her arms across her chest. She didn't want to get into a debate, but she thought Denver was rather nice, as well. "Nicer than Denver?"

He chuckled, as understanding lit his eyes. "Yes. Denver has its strong points—don't get me wrong—but there's something about Sydney that's unique. I'm not saying that just because it's where I was born."

"So what's so nice about it?"

He smiled again and, as if on cue, those sensations in her stomach fluttered and spread through her entire midsection.

"I hate to sound like a travel ad, but Australia is a cosmopolitan place drenched in history and surrounded by some of the most beautiful beaches imaginable. Close your eyes for a moment and envision this, Gemma."

She closed her eyes and he began talking in a soft tone, describing the beaches in detail. From his description, she could all but feel a spray of ocean water on her lips, a cool breeze caressing her skin.

"There're Kingscliff Beach, Byron Bay, Newcastle and Lord Howe, just to name a few. Each of them is an aquatic paradise, containing the purest blue-green waters your eyes can behold."

"Like the color of your eyes?" Her eyes were still closed.

She heard his soft chuckle. "Yes, somewhat. And speaking of eyes, you can open yours now."

She slowly lifted her lids to find his eyes right there. He had inched his head closer to hers and not only were his eyes right there, so were his lips. The thoughts that suddenly went racing through her mind were crazy, but all she would have to do was to stick out her tongue to taste his lips. That was a temptation she was having a hard time fighting.

Her breathing increased and she could tell by the rise and fall of his masculine chest, that so had his. Was there something significantly dangerous about flying this high in the sky that altered your senses? Zapped them real good and sent them reeling off course? Filled your mind with thoughts you wouldn't normally entertain?

If the answer to all those questions was a resounding yes, then that explained why her mind was suddenly filled with the thought of engaging in a romantic liaison with the man who was not only her client, but also her oldest brother's best friend.

"Gemma…" It seemed he had inched his mouth a little closer; so close she could feel his moist breath on her lips as he said her name in that deep Australian accent of his.

Instead of responding, she inched her mouth closer, too, as desire, the intensity of which she'd never felt before, made her entire body shiver with a need she didn't know she was capable of having. The green eyes locked on hers were successfully quashing any thoughts of pulling her mouth back before it was too late.

"Would either of you like some more snacks?"

Callum jumped and then quickly turned his face away from Gemma to glance up at the smiling flight attendant. He drew in a deep breath before responding. "No, thanks. I don't want anything."

He knew that was a lie the moment he'd said it. He *did* want something, but what he wanted only the woman sitting beside him could give.

The flight attendant then glanced over at Gemma and she responded in a shaky voice. "No, I'm fine."

It was only after the attendant had moved on that Callum glanced at Gemma. Her back was to him while she looked out the window. He suspected that she was going to pretend nothing had happened between them a few moments ago. There was no doubt in his mind that they would have kissed if the flight attendant hadn't interrupted them.

"Gemma?"

It took her longer than he felt was necessary to turn around and when she did, she immediately began talking about something that he couldn't have cared less about. "I was able to pack my color samples, Callum, so that you'll get an idea of what will best suit your home. I'll give you my suggestions, but of course the final decision will be yours. How do you like earth-tone colors? I'm thinking they will work best."

He fought the urge to say that what would work best would be to pick up where they'd left off, but instead he nodded and decided to follow her lead for now. In a way he felt good knowing that at least something had been accomplished today. She had finally become aware of him as a man. And he was giving her time to deal with that. He wouldn't push her, nor would he rush things for now. He would let nature take its course and with the degree of passion they exhibited a short while ago, he had no reason to think that it wouldn't.

"I happen to like earth-tone colors, so they will

probably work for me," he said, although he truly didn't give a royal damn. The bottom line was whatever she liked would work for him because he had every intention of her sharing that house with him.

"That's good, but I intend to provide you with a selection of vibrant colors, as well. Reds, greens, yellows and blues are the fashionable hues now. And we can always mix them up to create several bold splashes. Many people are doing that now."

She continued talking, and he would nod on occasion to pretend he was listening. If she needed to feel she was back in control of things, then so be it. He relaxed in his seat, tilted his head and watched ardently as her mouth moved while thinking what he would love doing to that mouth if given the chance. He decided to think positive and concentrated on what he would do with that mouth *when* he got the chance.

A few moments after Callum closed his eyes, Gemma stopped talking, satisfied that she had talked him to sleep. She had discussed some of everything with him regarding the decorating of his home to make sure they stayed on topic. The last thing she wanted was for him to bring up what almost happened between them. Just the thought of how close they'd come to sharing a kiss, right here on this airplane, had her pulse racing something awful.

She had never behaved inappropriately with a client before and wasn't sure exactly what had brought it on today. She would chalk it up as a weak moment when she'd almost yielded to temptation. When she had noticed just how close their mouths were, it had seemed a perfectly natural thing to want to taste his lips. Evidently, he'd felt the same way about hers, because his mouth had been inching toward hers with as much enthusiasm as hers had moved toward his. She was grateful for the flight attendant's timely interruption.

Had the woman suspected what they had been about to do? The thought had made Gemma's head heat up with embarrassment. Her heart was racing and the palms of her hands felt damp just thinking about it. She readjusted the pillow behind her head, knowing she would have to regain control of senses jolted by too much turbulence. Callum was just a man. He was a client. A friend of her family. He was not someone she should start thinking about in a sexual way.

She had gone twenty-four years without giving any man a second thought and going another twenty-four the same way suited her just fine.

Four

Gemma glanced around the spacious hotel where she and Callum would be staying for the night—in separate rooms, of course. Once their plane had landed, she had given herself a mental shake to make sure all her senses were back under control. Fortunately, the rest of the flight had been uneventful. Callum had kept his lips to himself and she had kept hers where they belonged. After a while, she had begun feeling comfortable around him again.

They'd taken a taxi from the airport. Callum had informed her that a private car service would arrive the next morning to take them to his parents' home. Gemma assumed they would be staying with his parents for the duration of the trip.

She thought this hotel was beautiful and would rival any of the major chains back home. The suite was spacious with floor-to-ceiling windows that looked out onto Sydney, which at this hour was dotted with bright lights.

Because she had slept a lot on the plane, she wasn't sleepy now. In fact, she was wide awake, although the clock on the nightstand by the bed indicated that it was after midnight. It was hard to believe that on the other side of the world in Denver they were trailing a day behind and it was eight in the morning.

She strolled to the window and looked out. She missed Denver already, but she couldn't help being fascinated by all the things she'd already seen. Although their plane had landed during the night hours, the taxi had taken them through many beautiful sections of the city that were lit up, and showed just how truthful Callum had been when he'd said that there was no place in the world quite like Sydney.

Gemma drew in a deep breath and tried to ignore a vague feeling of disappointment. Even though she was glad Callum hadn't mentioned their interrupted kiss, she hadn't expected him to completely ignore her. Although they'd shared conversation since, most of it had been with him providing details about Sydney and with her going over information about the decorating of his home. The thought that he could control his emotions around her so easily meant that, although he had been drawn to her for that one quick instant, he didn't think she was worth pursuing. If those were his thoughts, she should be grateful, instead of feeling teed off. Her disappointment and irritation just didn't make any sense.

She left the window and crossed the hotel room to the decorative mirror on the wall to study her features.

Okay, so she hadn't looked her best after the eighteen-hour plane flight, but she had taken a shower and had freshened up since then. Too bad he couldn't see her now. But overall, she hadn't looked awful.

Gemma couldn't help wondering what kind of woman would interest Callum. She was totally clueless. She'd never seen him with a woman before. She knew the types Zane and Derringer preferred dating—women who were all legs, beautiful, sophisticated, shallow, but easy to get into bed. For some reason she couldn't see Callum attracted to that type of woman.

There were times she wished she had a lot of experience with men and was not still a twenty-four-year-old virgin. There had been a number of times during her college days when guys had tried, although unsuccessfully, to get her into bed. When they had failed, they'd dubbed her "Ice Princess Gemma." That title hadn't bothered her in the least. She'd rather be known as an ice princess than an easy lay. She smiled, thinking that more than one frustrated stud had given up on seducing her. Giving up on her because she refused to put out was one thing, but ignoring her altogether was another.

A part of her knew the best thing to do was to relegate such thoughts to the back of her mind. It was better that he hadn't followed up on what had almost happened between them. But another part of her—the one that was a woman with as much vanity as any other female—hadn't liked it one bit and couldn't let it go.

A smile swept across her lips. Callum had suggested that they meet in the morning for breakfast before the car arrived to take them to his parents' home. That was fine with her, because she would be meeting his parents and she wanted to look her best. The last thing she wanted was for them to think he'd hired someone who didn't know how to dress professionally. So tomorrow she would get rid of her usual attire of jeans and a casual top and wear something a little more becoming.

She would see just how much Callum could ignore her then.

Callum got up the next morning feeling as tired as he'd been when he went to bed past midnight. He had tossed and turned most of the night, frustrated that he hadn't taken the opportunity to taste Gemma's lips when the chance to do so had been presented to him.

Every part of his body hardened with the memory of a pair of luscious lips that had been barely a breath away from his. And when she had tilted her head even more to him, placing her lips within a tongue reach, he had felt the lower part of his body throb.

The desire that had flowed between them had been anything but one-sided. Charged sensations as strong as any electrical current had surged through both their bodies and he had fought back the urge to unsnap her seat belt and pull her into his lap while lapping her mouth with everything he had.

He remembered the conversations they'd shared and how she'd tried staying on course by being the consummate professional. While she'd been talking, his gaze had been fixated on her mouth. He couldn't recall a woman who could look both sexy and sweet at the same time, as well as hot and cool when the mood suited her. He loved all the different facets of Gemma, and he planned on being a vital part of each one of them. How could any man not want to?

Minutes later, after taking a shower and getting dressed, he left his hotel room to walk a few doors down to where Gemma had spent the night. Just the thought that she had been sleeping so close had done something to him. He wondered if she had gotten a good night's sleep. Or had she tossed and turned most of the night, as he had? Probably not. He figured she had no idea what sexual frustration was all about. And if she did, he didn't want to know about it, especially if some other man ruled her thoughts.

The possibility of that didn't sit well with him, since he couldn't handle the thought of Gemma with any other man but him. He pulled in a deep breath before lifting his hand to knock on her door.

"Who is it?"

"Callum."

"Just a moment."

While waiting, he turned to study the design of the wallpaper that covered the expanse of the wall that led to the elevator. It was a busy design, but he had to admit that it matched the carpet perfectly, pulling in colors he would not have normally paid attention to.

He shook his head, remembering that Gemma had gone on and on about different colors and how her job would be to coordinate them to play off each other. He was surprised that he could recall any of her words when the only thoughts going through his mind had been what he'd like doing to her physically.

"Come on in, Callum. I just need to grab a jacket," she said upon opening the door.

He turned around and immediately sucked in a deep breath. He had to lean against the doorframe to keep from falling. *His* Gemma wasn't wearing jeans and a top today. Instead, she was dressed in a tan-colored skirt that flowed to her ankles, a pair of chocolate-suede, medium-heeled shoes and a printed blouse. Seeing her did something to every muscle, every cell and every pore of his body. And his gut twisted in a knot. She looked absolutely stunning. Even her hair was different. Rather than wearing it in a ponytail she had styled it to hang down to her shoulders.

He'd only seen her a few other times dressed like this, and that had been when they'd run into each other at church. He entered the room and closed the door behind him, feeling a gigantic tug in his chest as he watched her move around the room. He became enmeshed in her movements and how graceful and fluid they were.

"Did you get a good night's sleep, Callum?"

He blinked when he noticed that she stood staring at him, smiling. Was he imagining things or did he see amusement curving her lips? "I'm sorry, what did you ask?"

"I wanted to know if you got a good night's sleep. I'm sure it felt good being back home."

He thought about what she said and although he could agree that it was good being back home, it felt even better having her here with him. He'd thought about this a number of times, dreamed that he would share his homeland with her. He had six weeks and he intended to make every second, minute and hour count.

Apparently, she was waiting for his response. "Sleep didn't come easy. I guess I'm suffering from jet lag. And, yes, I'm glad to be home," he said, checking his watch. "Ready to go down for breakfast?"

"Yes, I'm starving."

"I can imagine. You didn't eat a whole lot on the plane."

She chuckled. "Only because I wasn't sure I could keep it down. There was a lot of turbulence."

And he'd known how much that bothered her. He was glad when she'd finally been able to sleep through it. He had watched her most of the time while she'd done so.

"I'm ready now, Callum."

He was tempted to reach out and take her hand in his, but he knew that doing such a thing would not be a smart move right now. He needed her to get to know him, not as her brother's best friend, but as the man who would always be a part of her life.

"Hey, don't look at my plate like that. I told you I was hungry," Gemma said, laughing. Her stack of pancakes was just as high as Callum's. He had told her this particular hotel, located in downtown Sydney, was known to serve the best pancakes. They not only served the residents of the hotel but locals who dropped in on their way to work. From where Gemma sat, she could see the Sydney Harbour Bridge in the distance. It was a beautiful sight.

"Trust me, I understand. I remember my mom bringing me here as a kid when I did something good in school," he said while pouring syrup onto his pancakes.

"Wow, you mean this hotel is *that* old?" Her eyes twinkled with mischief.

He glanced over at her as amusement flickered in his gaze. "Old? Just what are you trying to say, Gemma?"

"Umm, nothing. Sorry. I have to remember that you're my client and I have to watch what I say. The last thing I want to do is offend you."

"And be careful that you don't," he warned, chuckling. "Or all that information you provided yesterday on colors and designs would have been for naught. How you can keep that stuff straight in your head is beyond me."

He paused a moment. "And I talked to Ramsey last night. Everything is fine back in Denver and I assured him all was well here."

Gemma smiled as she took a sip of her coffee. "Did you tell him we were on the flight from hell getting here?"

"Not quite in those words, but I think he got the idea. He asked me if you fainted when the plane hit the first pocket of turbulence."

She made a face. "Funny. Did he mention how Chloe is doing?"

"Yes, she's fine, just can't wait for November to roll around." He smiled. "She has two more months to go."

"I started to call them last night when we got in, but after I took a shower and went to bed that did it for me. I hadn't thought I'd be able to sleep so soundly, but I did."

During the rest of their meal, Gemma explained to him how they managed to pull off a surprise baby shower for Chloe last month right under her sister-in-law's nose, and how, although Ramsey and Chloe didn't want to know the sex of the baby before it was born,

Megan, Bailey and she were hoping for a girl, while Zane, Derringer and the twins were anticipating a boy.

Sipping coffee and sharing breakfast with Callum seemed so natural. She hadn't ever shared breakfast with him before…at least not when it had been just the two of them. Occasionally, they would arrive at Ramsey's place for breakfast at about the same time, but there had always been other family members around. She found him fun to talk to and felt good knowing he had noticed her outfit and even complimented her on how she looked. She had caught him staring at her a few times, which meant he couldn't ignore her so easily after all.

They had finished breakfast and were heading back toward the elevators when suddenly someone called out.

"Callum, it's you! I can't believe you're home!"

Both Callum and Gemma glanced around at the same time a woman threw herself at him and proceeded to wrap her arms around his waist while placing a generous smack on his lips.

"Meredith! It's good to see you," Callum said, trying to pry himself from the woman's grip. Once that was accomplished, he smiled pleasantly at the dark-haired female who was smiling up at him like an adoring fan. "What are you doing in town so early?"

The woman laughed. "I'm meeting some friends for breakfast." It was then that she turned and regarded Gemma. "Oh, hello."

The first thought that came into Gemma's mind was that the woman was simply beautiful. The second was that if it was the woman's intent to pretend she was just noticing Gemma's presence, then she had failed miserably, since there was no way she could have missed her, when she'd nearly knocked her down getting to Callum.

"Meredith, I'd love you to meet a good friend of mine," he said, reaching out, catching Gemma's hand and pulling her closer to his side. "Gemma Westmoreland. Gemma, this is Meredith Kenton. Meredith's father and mine are old school chums."

Gemma presented her hand to the woman when it became obvious the woman was not going to extend hers. "Meredith."

Meredith hesitated a second before taking it. "So, you're from the States, Gemma?"

"Yes."

"Oh."

She then turned adoring eyes on Callum again, and Gemma didn't miss the way the woman's gaze lit up when Callum smiled at her. "Now that you're back home, Callum, what about us doing dinner at the Oasis, going sailing and having a picnic on the beach."

For crying out loud. Will you let the man at least catch his breath, Gemma wanted to scream, refusing to consider that she was feeling a bit jealous. *And besides, for all you know, I might be his woman and if I were I wouldn't let him do any of those things with you. Talk about blatant disrespect.*

"I'm going to be tied up this visit," Callum said, easing Gemma closer to his side. Gemma figured he was trying to paint a picture for Meredith that really wasn't true—that they were a twosome. Any other time she might have had a problem with a man insinuating such a thing, but in this case she didn't mind. In fact, she welcomed the opportunity to pull the rug right out from under Miss Disrespect. Meredith was obviously one of those "pushy" women.

"And I'm only back home for a short while," he added.

"Please don't tell me you're going back over there."

"Yes, I am."

"When are you coming home for good?" Meredith pouted, her thin lips exuding disappointment.

Gemma looked up at Callum, a questioning look in her eyes. Was this the woman waiting for him that he told her didn't exist? He met her gaze and as if he read the question lingering there, he pulled her even closer to his side. "I'm not sure. I kind of like it over there. As you know, Mom is an American, so I'm fortunate to have family on both continents."

"Yes, but your home is here."

He smiled as he glanced down at Gemma. He then looked back at Meredith. "Home is where the heart is."

The woman then turned a cold, frosty gaze on Gemma. "And he brought you back with him."

Before Gemma could respond, Callum spoke up. "Yes, I brought her back with me to meet my parents."

Gemma knew the significance of that statement, even if it was a lie. To say he had brought her home to meet his parents meant there was a special relationship between them. In truth, that wasn't the case but for some reason he didn't want Meredith to know that, and in a way she didn't want Meredith to know it, either.

"Well, I see my friends have arrived now," she said in a cutting tone. "Gemma, I hope you enjoy your time here in Sydney and, Callum, I'll talk to you later." The woman then beat a hasty retreat.

With his hand on her arm, Callum steered Gemma toward the elevator. Once they were alone inside the elevator, Gemma spoke. "Why did you want Meredith to assume we were an item?"

He smiled down at her. "Do you have a problem with that?"

Gemma shook her head. "No, but why?"

He stared at her for a few moments, opened his mouth to say something, then closed it. He seemed to think for a minute. "Just because."

She lifted a brow. "Just because?"

"Yes, just because."

She frowned up at him. "I'd like more of a reason than that, Callum. Is Meredith one of your former girl-friends?"

"Not officially. And before you assume the worst about me, I never gave her a reason to think anything between us was official or otherwise. I never led her on. She knew where she stood with me and I with her."

So it was one of those kinds of relationships, Gemma mused. The kind her brothers were notorious for. The kind that left the woman broken down and broken-hearted.

"And before you start feeling all indignant on Meredith's behalf, don't waste your time. Her first choice of the Austells was my brother, Colin. They dated for a few years and one day he walked in and found her in bed with another man."

"Oh." Gemma hadn't liked the woman from the first, and now she liked her even less.

The elevator stopped. They stepped off and Callum turned to her and placed his hand on her arm so she wouldn't go any farther. She hadn't expected the move and sensations escalated up her rib cage from his touch.

"I want to leave you with something to think about, Gemma," he said in that voice she loved hearing.

"What?"

"I know that watching your brothers and cousins operate with girls has colored your opinion of men in general. I think it's sad that their exploits have left a negative impression on you and I regret that. I won't speak for your brothers, because they can do that for themselves, but I can speak for myself. I'd never intentionally hurt any woman. It's my belief that I have a soul mate out there somewhere."

She lifted a brow. "A soul mate?"

"Yes."

Gemma couldn't help but wonder if such a thing really existed. She would be the first to admit that her cousin Dillon's first wife hadn't blended in well with the family, nor had she been willing to make any sacrifices for the man she loved. With his current wife, Pam, it was a different story. From the moment the family had met Pam, they'd known she was a godsend. The same thing held true for Chloe. Gemma, Megan and Bailey had bonded with their sister-in-law immediately, even before she and Ramsey had married. And just to see the two couples together, you would know they were meant for each other and loved each other deeply.

So Gemma knew true love worked for some people, but she wasn't willing to suffer any heartbreak while on a quest to find Mr. Right or her soul mate. But as far as Callum was concerned, she was curious about one thing. "And you really believe you have a soul mate?"

"Yes."

She noted that he hadn't hesitated in answering. "How will you know when you meet her?"

"I'll know."

He sounded pretty confident about that, she thought. She shrugged. "Well, good luck in finding her," she said as they exited the building and headed toward the parking garage.

She noted that Callum appeared to have considered her comment, and then he tilted his head and smiled at her. "Thanks. I appreciate that."

Five

"Wow, this car is gorgeous, but I thought a private car was coming for us."

Callum looked over at Gemma and smiled as they walked toward the car parked in the hotel's parking garage. "I decided to have my car brought to me instead."

"This is your car?" Gemma studied the beautiful, shiny black two-seater sports car.

He chuckled as he opened the door for her. "Yes, this baby is mine." *And so are you,* he wanted to say as he watched her slide her legs into the car, getting a glimpse of her beautiful calves and ankles. "I've had it now for a few years."

She glanced up at him. "Weren't you ever tempted to ship it to Denver?"

"No," he said with a smile. "Can you imagine me

driving something like this around Ramsey's sheep farm?"

"No, I can't," she said, grinning when he got in on the other side and snapped his seat belt into place. "Is it fast?"

"Oh, yes. And you'll see that it has a smooth ride."

Callum knew she was sold on the car's performance moments later when they hit the open highway and she settled back in her seat. He used to imagine things being just like this, with him driving this car around town with the woman he loved sitting in the passenger seat beside him.

He glanced over at her for a second and saw how closely she was paying attention to everything they passed, as if she didn't want to miss anything. He drew in a deep breath, inhaling her scent right along with it, and felt desire settle into his bones. Nothing new there; he'd wanted Gemma since the first time he'd seen her and knew she would be his.

"This place is simply beautiful, Callum."

He smiled, pleased that she thought so. "More so than Denver?"

She threw her head back and laughed. "Hey, there's no place like home. I love Denver."

"I know." Just as he knew it would be hard getting her to leave Denver to move to Sydney with him. He would have returned home long ago, but he'd been determined not to until he had her with him.

"We're on our way to your parents' home?" she asked, interrupting his thoughts.

"Yes. They're looking forward to meeting you."

Surprise swept across her face. "Really? Why?"

He wished he could tell her the truth, but decided to say something else equally true. "You're Ramsey's sister. Your brother made an impression on them during the six months he lived here. They consider him like another son."

"He adores them, as well. Your family is all he used to write us about while he was here. I was away at college and his letters used to be so full of adventure. I knew then that he'd made the right decision to turn over the running of the family's real-estate firm to Dillon and pursue his dream of becoming a sheep rancher. Just as my father always wanted to do."

He heard the touch of pain in her voice and sensed that mentioning her father had brought back painful memories. "You were close to him, weren't you?"

When they came to a snag in traffic, he watched her moisten her lips before replying to his question. "Yes. I was definitely a daddy's girl, but then so were Megan and Bailey. He was super. I can still recall that day Dillon and Ramsey showed up to break the news to us. They had been away at college, and when I saw them come in together I knew something was wrong. But I never imagined the news they were there to deliver."

She paused a moment. "The pain wouldn't have been so great had we not lost our parents and Uncle Adam and Aunt Clarisse at the same time. I'll never forget how alone I felt, and how Dillon and Ramsey promised that, no matter what, they would keep us together. And they did. Because Dillon was the oldest, he became the head of the family and Ramsey, only seven months younger, became second in charge. Together they pulled off what some thought would be impossible."

Callum recalled hearing the story a number of times from Ramsey. He had hesitated about going to Australia because he hadn't wanted to leave everything on Dillon's shoulders, so he'd waited until Bailey had finished high school and started college before taking off for Australia.

"I'm sure your parents would be proud of all of you," he said.

She smiled. "Yes, I'm sure they would be, as well. Dillon and Ramsey did an awesome job and I know for sure we were a handful at times, some of us more than others."

He knew she was thinking about her cousin, Bane, and all the trouble he used to get into. Now Brisbane Westmoreland was in the Navy with dreams of becoming a SEAL.

Callum checked his watch. "We won't be long now. Knowing Mom, she'll have a feast for lunch."

A smile touched Gemma's lips. "I'm looking forward to meeting your parents, especially your mother, the woman who captured your father's heart."

He returned her smile, while thinking that his mother was looking forward to meeting her—the woman who'd captured his.

Surprise swept across Gemma's face when Callum brought his car to the marker denoting the entrance to his family's ranch. She leaned forward in her seat to glance around through the car's windows. She was spellbound, definitely at a loss for words. The ranch, the property it sat on and the land surrounding it were breathtaking.

The first thing she noticed was that this ranch was

a larger version of her brother's, but the layout was identical. "I gather that Ramsey's design of the Shady Tree Ranch was based on this one," she said.

Callum nodded. "Yes, he fell in love with this place and when he went back home he designed his ranch as a smaller replica of this one, down to every single detail, even to the placement of where the barns, shearing plants and lambing stations are located."

"No wonder you weren't in a hurry to return back here. Being at the Shady Tree Ranch was almost home away from home for you. There were so many things to remind you of this place. But then, on the other hand, if it had been me, seeing a smaller replica of my home would have made me homesick."

He keyed in the code that would open the electronic gate while thinking that the reason he had remained in Denver after helping Ramsey set up his ranch, and the reason he'd never gotten homesick, were basically the same. Gemma. He hadn't wanted to leave her behind and return to Australia, and he hadn't, except for the occasional holiday visit. And he truly hadn't missed home because, as he'd told Meredith, home is where the heart is and his heart had always been with Gemma, whether she knew it or not.

He put the car in gear and drove down the path leading to his parents' ranch house. The same place where he'd lived all his life before moving into his own place at twenty-three, right out of college. But it hadn't been unusual to sleep over while working the ranch with his father and brothers. He had many childhood memories of walks along this same path, then bicycle rides, motorcycle rides and finally rides behind the wheel of a car. It felt good to be home—even better that he hadn't come alone.

He fully expected not only his parents to be waiting inside the huge ranch house, but his brothers and their wives, and his sister and brother-in-law as well. Everyone was eager to meet the woman whose pull had kept him working in North America as Ramsey's ranch manager for three years. And everyone was sworn to secrecy, since they knew how important it was for him to win Gemma's heart on his turf.

She was about to start getting to know the real Callum Austell. The man she truly belonged to.

When Callum brought the car to a stop in front of the sprawling home, the front door opened and a smiling older couple walked out. Gemma knew immediately that they were his parents. They were a beautiful couple. A perfect couple. Soul mates. Another thing she noted was that Callum had the older man's height and green eyes and had the woman's full lips, high cheekbones and dimpled smile.

And then, to Gemma's surprise, following on the older couple's heels were three men and three women. It was easy to see who in the group were Callum's brothers and his sister. It was uncanny just how much they favored their parents.

"Seems like you're going to get to meet everyone today, whether you're ready to do so or not," Callum said.

Gemma released a chuckle. "Hey, I have a big family, too. I remember how it was when I used to come home after being away at college. Everyone is glad to see you come home. Besides, you're your parents' baby."

He threw his head back and laughed. "Baby? At thirty-four, I don't think so."

"I do. Once a baby always a baby. Just ask Bailey."

Just a look into his green eyes let her know he still wasn't buying it. He smiled as he opened the door to get out and said, "Just get ready for the Austells."

By the time Callum had rounded the car to open the door for her to get out, his parents, siblings and in-laws were there and she could tell that everyone was glad to see him. Moments later she stood, leaning against the side of his car, and watched all the bear hugs he was receiving, thinking there was nothing quite like returning home to a family who loved you.

"Mom, Dad, everyone, I would like you to meet Gemma Westmoreland." He reached out his hand to her and she glanced over at him a second before moving away from the car to join him where he stood with his family.

"So you're Gemma," Le'Claire Austell said, smiling after giving Gemma a hug. "I've heard quite a lot about you."

Surprise lit up Gemma's features. "You have?"

The woman smiled brightly. "Of course I have. Ramsey adores his siblings and would share tales with us about you, Megan, Bailey and your brothers, as well as all the other Westmorelands all the time. I think talking about all of you made missing you while he was here a little easier."

Gemma nodded and then she was pulled into Callum's dad's arms for a hug and was introduced to everyone present. There was Callum's oldest brother, Morris, and his wife, Annette, and his brother, Colin, and his wife, Mira. His only sister Le'Shaunda, whom everyone called Shaun, and her husband, Donnell.

"You'll get to meet our three grands at dinner," Callum's mom was saying.

"I'm looking forward to it," Gemma replied warmly.

While everyone began heading inside the house, Callum touched Gemma's arm to hold her back. "Is something wrong?" He looked at her with concern in his green eyes. "I saw the way you looked at me when I called you over to meet everyone."

Gemma quickly looked ahead at his family, who were disappearing into the house and then back at Callum. "You didn't tell your family why I'm here."

"I didn't have to. They know why you're here." He studied her features for a moment. "What's going on in that head of yours, Gemma Westmoreland? What's bothering you?"

She shrugged, suddenly feeling silly for even bringing it up. "Nothing. I just remember what you insinuated with Meredith and hoped you weren't going to give your family the same impression."

"That you and I have something going on?"

"Yes."

He watched her for a moment and then touched her arm gently. "Hey, relax. My family knows the real deal between us, trust me. I thought you understood why I pulled that stunt with Meredith."

"I do. Look, let's forget I brought it up. It's just that your family is so nice."

He chuckled and pulled her to him. "We're Aussies, eight originals and one convert. We can't help but be nice."

She tossed him a grin before easing away. "So you say." She then looked over at the car as she headed up the steps to the house. "Do you need help getting our luggage?"

"No. We aren't staying here."

She turned around so quickly she missed her step and he caught her before she tumbled. "Be careful, Gemma."

She shook her head, trying to ignore how close they were standing and why she suddenly felt all kinds of sensations flooding her insides. "I'm okay. But why did you say we're not staying here?"

"Because we're not."

She went completely still. "But—but you said we were staying at your home."

He caught her chin in his fingers and met her gaze. "We are. This is not my home. This is my parents' home."

She swallowed, confused. "I thought your home is what I'm decorating. Isn't it empty?"

"*That* house is, but I also own a condo on the beach. That's where we're staying while we're here. Do you have a problem with that, Gemma?"

Gemma forced herself to breathe when it became clear that she and Callum would be sharing living space while she was here. Why did the thought of that bother her?

She had to admit for the first time she was noticing things about him she'd never noticed before. And she was experiencing things around him that she hadn't experienced before. Like the way she was swept up in heated desire and the sensuous tickling in the pit of her stomach whenever he was within a few feet of her, like now...

"Gemma?"

She swallowed again as she met his gaze and the green eyes were holding hers with an intensity that she wasn't used to. She gave her head a mental shake. His family had to be wondering why they were still outside. She had to get real. She was here to do a job and she would do it without having these crazy thoughts that Callum was after her body, just because she'd begun having crazy fantasies about him.

"No, I don't have a problem with that." She pulled away from him and smiled. "Come on, your parents are probably wondering why we're still out here," she said, moving ahead and making an attempt to walk up the steps again.

She succeeded and kept walking toward the door, fully aware that he was watching every step she took.

Callum glanced around his parents' kitchen and drew in a deep breath. So far, things were going just as he'd hoped. From the masked smiles and nods he'd gotten from his family, he knew they agreed with his assessment of Gemma—that she was a precious gem. Even his three nephews, ages six, eight and ten, who were usually shy with strangers, had warmed up to her.

He knew that, for a brief moment, she had been confused as to why his family had taken so readily to her. What he'd told her hadn't been a lie. They knew the reason she was here and decorating that house he had built was only part of it. In fact, a minor part.

"When are you getting a haircut?"

Callum turned and smiled at his father. "I could ask you the same thing." Todd Austell's hair was just as long as his son's and Callum couldn't remember him ever getting his hair cut. In fact, it appeared longer now than the last time he'd seen it.

"Don't hold your breath for that to happen," his father said with joking amusement in his green gaze. "I love my golden locks. The only thing I love more is your mother."

Callum leaned against the kitchen counter. His mother, sister and sisters-in-law had Gemma in a corner and from their expressions he knew they were making *his woman* feel right at home. His brother and brothers-in-law were outside manning the grills, and his nephews were somewhere playing ball. His parents had decided to have a family cookout to welcome him and Gemma home.

"Gemma is a nice girl, Callum. Le'Claire and Shaun like her."

He could tell. He glanced up at his father. "And you?"

A smile crossed Todd Austell's lips. "I like her."

As if she felt Callum's gaze, she glanced over in his direction and smiled. His muscles tightened in desire for her.

"Dad?"

"Yes?"

"After you met Mom and knew she was the woman for you, how long did it take you to convince her of it?"

"Too long."

Callum chuckled. "How long was too long?"

"A few months. Remember, I had an engagement to break off and then your mother assumed that flying was her life. I had to convince her that she was sorely mistaken about that, and that I was her life."

Callum shook his head. His father was something else. Callum's was one of the wealthiest families in Sydney; the Austells had made their millions not only in sheep farming but also in the hotel industry. The hotel where he and Gemma had stayed last night was part of just one of several hotel chains that Colin was in charge of. Morris was vice president of the sheep-farm operation.

When Callum was home, he worked wherever he was needed, but he enjoyed sheep farming more. In fact, he was CEO of his own ranching firm, which operated several sheep ranches in Australia. Each was run by an efficient staff. He also owned a vast amount of land in Australia. He'd never been one to flaunt his wealth, although in his younger days he'd been well aware money was what had driven a lot of women to him. He had frustrated a number of them by being an elusive catch.

He glanced again at the group of women together and then at his father. "I guess it worked."

The older man lifted a brow. "What worked?"

"You were able to convince Mom that you were her life."

A deep smile touched his father's lips. "Four kids and three grandsons later, what can I say?"

A smile just as deep touched Callum's lips. "You can say that in the end Mom became your life as well. Because I think it's obvious that she has."

Six

The moment Gemma snapped her seat belt in place, a bright smile curved her lips. "Your family is simply wonderful, Callum, and I especially like your mom. She's super."

"Yes, she is," Callum agreed as he started the car's engine to leave his parents' home.

"And your dad adores her."

Callum chuckled. "You can tell?"

"How could I not? I think it's wonderful."

She was quiet for a moment. "I recall my parents being that way, having a close relationship and all. As I got older, although I missed them both, I couldn't imagine one living without the other, so I figured that if they had to die, I was glad they at least went together," she said.

Gemma forced back the sadness that wanted to cloud

what had been a great day. She glanced over at Callum. "And I love your parents' home. It's beautiful. Your mother mentioned that she did all the decorating."

"She did."

"Then why didn't you get her to decorate yours?"

"Mine?"

"Yes, the one you've hired me to do. I'm grateful that you thought of me, mind you, but your mother could have done it."

"Yes, she could have, but she doesn't have the time. Taking care of my dad is a full-time job. She spoils him rotten."

Gemma laughed. "Appears he likes spoiling her as well."

She had enjoyed watching the older couple displaying such a warm, loving attitude toward each other. It was obvious that their children were used to seeing them that way. Gemma also thought Callum's three nephews were little cuties.

"Is it far to the condo where you live?" she asked him, settling back against the car seat. When they walked out of Callum's parents' house, she noted that the evening temperature had dropped and it was cool. It reminded her of Denver just weeks before the first snowfall in late September. She then remembered that Australia's seasons were opposite the ones in North America.

"No, we'll be there in around twenty minutes. Are you tired?"

"Umm. Jet lag I think."

"Probably is. Go ahead and rest your eyes for a while."

Gemma took him up on his offer and closed her eyes

for a moment. Callum was right, the reason she wanted to rest had to do with jet lag. She would probably feel this way until she adjusted to the change in time zone.

She tried to clear her mind of any thoughts, but found it impossible to do when she was drawn back to the time she had spent at Callum's parents' home. What she'd told him was true. She had enjoyed herself and thought his family was wonderful. They reminded her of her siblings.

She was close to her siblings and cousins, and they teased each other a lot. She'd picked up on the love between Callum and his siblings. He was the youngest and it was obvious that they cared deeply about him and were protective of him.

More than once, while talking to Callum's mom, she had felt his eyes on her and had glanced across the room to have her gaze snagged by his. Had she imagined it or had she seen male interest lurking in their green depths?

There had been times when the perfection of Callum's features had nearly stopped her in her tracks and she found herself at several standstills today. Both of his brothers were handsome, but in her book, Callum was gorgeous, and was even more so for some reason today. She could understand the likes of Meredith trying to come on to him. Back in Denver on the ranch, he exuded the air of a hardworking roughneck, but here in Sydney, dressed in a pair of slacks and a dress shirt and driving a sports car, he passed the test as the hot, sexy and sophisticated man that he was. If only all those women back in Denver could see him now.

She slowly opened her eyes and studied his profile

over semi-lowered lashes as he drove the car. Sitting in a perfect posture, he radiated the kind of a strength most men couldn't fabricate, even on their best days. His hair appeared chestnut in color in the evening light and hung around his shoulders in fluid waves.

There was something about him that infused a degree of warmth all through her. Why hadn't she felt it before? Maybe she had, but had forced herself to ignore it. And then there was the difference in their ages. He was ten years her senior. The thought of dating a man in close proximity to her age was bad enough; to consider one older, she'd thought, would be asking for trouble, definitely way out of her league.

Her gaze moved to his hands. She recalled on more than one occasion seeing those hands that were now gripping the steering wheel handle the sheep on her brother's ranch. There was an innate strength about them that extended all the way to his clean and short fingernails.

According to Megan, you could tell a lot about a man by his hands. That might be true, but Gemma didn't have a clue what she should be looking for. It was at times like this that her innocence bothered her. For once—maybe twice—she wouldn't mind knowing how it felt to get lost in the depth of a male's embrace, kissed by him in a way that could curl her toes and shoot sparks of pleasure all threw her. She wanted to be made love to by a man who knew what he was doing. A man who would make her first time special, something she would remember for the rest of her life and not forget when the encounter was over.

She closed her eyes again and remembered that

moment on the plane when Callum had awakened and found her there, close to his face and staring at him. She remembered how he had stared back, how she had actually felt a degree of lust she hadn't thought she could feel and a swell of desire that had nearly shaken her to the core. She had felt mesmerized by his gaze, had felt frozen in a trance, and the only thing that would break it would be a kiss. And they had come seconds, inches from sharing one.

She knew it would have to be one of those kisses she'd always dreamed of sharing with a man. The kind that for some reason she believed only Callum Austell could deliver. Yes, the mind-blowing, toe-curling kind. A ripple of excitement sent shivers up her spine at the thought of being swept up in Callum's embrace, kissed by him, made love to by him.

She sucked in a quick breath, wondering what was making her think such things. What was causing her to have such lurid thoughts? And then she knew. She was attracted to her brother's best friend in the worst possible way. And as the sound of the car's powerful engine continued to roar under Callum's skillful maneuvering on the roadway, she felt herself fall deeper and deeper into a deep sleep with thoughts of Callum Austell getting embedded thoroughly into her mind.

Callum settled comfortably in the driver's seat as he drove the road with the power and ease he had missed over the years. Three in fact. Although he had returned home on occasion and had taken the car on the road for good measure whenever he did, there was something different about it this time. Because he had his future wife sitting beside him.

He smiled when he quickly glanced at her before returning his gaze to the road. She was *sleeping* beside him. He couldn't wait for the time when she would be sleeping with him. The thought of having her in his arms, making love to every inch of her body, filled him with a desire he didn't know it was possible to feel. But then Gemma had always done that to him, even when she hadn't known she was doing it.

Over the years he'd schooled himself well, and very few knew how he felt. Ramsey and Dillon knew, of course, and he figured Zane and Derringer suspected something as well. What had probably given Callum away was his penchant for watching Gemma the way a fox watched the henhouse, with his eye on one unsuspecting hen. It wasn't surprising that Gemma was totally clueless.

So far things were going as planned, although there had been a few close calls with his family when he thought one of them would slip and give something away. He wanted Gemma to feel comfortable around him and his family, and the last thing he wanted was for her to feel as if she'd deliberately been set up in any way. He wanted her to feel a sense of freedom here that he believed she wouldn't feel back in Denver.

For her to want to try new and different things, to embrace herself as a woman, topped his list. And for the first time, he would encourage her to indulge all her desires with a man. But not just any man. With him. He wanted her to see that not all men had only one thing in mind when it came to a woman, and for two people to desire each other wasn't a bad thing.

He wanted her to understand and accept that no matter what happened between them, it would be okay because nothing they shared would be for the short term. He intended to make this forever.

Callum pulled into the gated condo community and drove directly to his home, which sat on a secluded stretch of beach, prized for the privacy he preferred. He planned to keep this place even after their home was fully decorated and ready to move in. But first he had to convince Gemma that he was worth it for her to leave the country where she'd been born, the country in which her family resided, and move here with him, to his side of the world.

He brought his car to a stop and killed the ignition. It was then that he turned toward her, keeping one hand on the steering wheel and draping the other across the back of the passenger seat. She looked beautiful, sleeping as if she didn't have a care in the world—and in a way she didn't. He would shoulder whatever problems she had from here on out.

With an analytical eye he studied her features. She was smiling while she slept and he wondered why. What pleasing thoughts were going through her mind? It had gotten dark, and the lights from the fixtures in front of his home cast a glow on her face at an angle that made it look even more beautiful. He could imagine having a little girl with her mouth and cheekbones, or a son with her ears and jaw. He thought she had cute ears.

With a tentative hand he reached out and brushed his fingers gently across her cheeks. She shifted and began mumbling something. He leaned closer to catch what she was saying and his gut tightened in a ball of ravenous desire when she murmured in her sleep, "Kiss me, Callum."

Gemma felt herself drowning in a sea of desire she'd never felt before. She and Callum were not on the ranch in Denver, but were back on the plane. This time the entire plane was empty. They were the only two people onboard.

He had adjusted their seats to pull her into his arms, but instead of kissing her he was torturing her mouth inside, nibbling from corner to corner, then taking his tongue and licking around the lines of her lips.

She moaned deep in her throat. She was ready for him to take her mouth and stop toying with it. She needed to feel his tongue sucking on hers, tasting it instead of teasing it, and then she wanted their tongues to tangle in a delirious and sensual duel.

She began mumbling words, telling him to stop toying with her and asking that he finish what he'd started. She wanted the kiss she'd almost gotten before—a kiss to lose herself in sensual pleasure. Close to her ear she heard a masculine growl, sensed the passion of a man wanting to mate and breathed in the scent of a hot male.

Then suddenly she felt herself being gently shaken. "Gemma. Wake up, Gemma."

She lifted drowsy lids only to find Callum's face right there in front of hers. Just as it had been on the plane. Just as it had been moments earlier in her dream. "Callum?"

"Yes," he replied in a warm voice that sent delicious shivers up her spine. His mouth was so close she could taste his breath on her lips. "Do you really want me to kiss you, Gemma? You are one Westmoreland that I'll give whatever you want."

Seven

Gemma forced the realization into her mind that she wasn't dreaming. This was the real deal. She was awake in Callum's car and he was leaning over her with his face close to hers and there wasn't a flight attendant to interrupt them if he decided to inch his mouth even closer. Would he?

That brought her back to his question. Did she want him to kiss her? Evidently, she had moaned out the request in her sleep and he'd heard it. From the look in the depth of his green eyes, he was ready to act on it. Is that what she wanted? He did say he would give her whatever she wanted.

More than anything, she wanted to be kissed by him. Although it wouldn't be her first kiss, she believed it would be the first one she received with a semblance of passion and desire on both sides. Before guys had wanted to kiss her, but she hadn't really cared if she kissed them or not.

This time she would act first and worry about the consequences of her actions later.

Holding his gaze, she whispered against his lips, "Yes, I want you to kiss me." She saw him smiling and giving a small nod of satisfaction before he leaned in closer. Before she could catch her next breath, he seized her mouth with his.

The first thing he did was seek out her tongue and the moment he captured it in his, she was a goner. He started off slow, plying her with a deep, thorough kiss as if he wanted to get acquainted with the taste and texture of her mouth, flicking the tip of his tongue all over the place, touching places she hadn't known a tongue could reach, while stirring up even more passion buried deep within her bones.

For a timeless moment, heat flooded her body in a way it had never done before, triggering her breasts to suddenly feel tender and the area between her thighs to throb. How could one man's kiss deliver so much pleasure? Elicit things from her she never knew existed?

Before she could dwell on any answers to her questions, he deepened the kiss and began mating with her mouth with an intensity and hunger that made her stomach muscles quiver. It was a move she felt all the way to her toes. She felt herself becoming feverish, hot and needy. When it came to a man, she'd never been needy.

He slanted his head, taking the kiss deeper still, while tangling with her tongue in a way she had dreamed about only moments earlier. But now she was getting the real thing and not mere snippets of a fantasy. He wasn't holding back on anything and his tongue was playing havoc with her senses in the process. It was a work of art, a sensuous skill. The way he'd managed to wrap his tongue around hers, only letting it go when it pleased him and capturing it again when he was ready to dispense even more pleasurable torture.

She had asked for this kiss and wasn't disappointed. Far from it. He was taking her over the edge in a way that would keep her falling with pleasure. His mouth seemed to fit hers perfectly, no matter what angle he took. And the more it plowed her mouth hungrily, the more every part of her body came alive in a way she wasn't used to.

She moaned deep in her throat when she felt the warmth of his fingers on her bare thigh and wondered when had he slid his hand under her skirt. When those fingers began inching toward her center, instinctively she shifted her body closer to his. The move immediately parted her thighs.

As if his fingers were fully aware of the impact they were having on her, they moved to stake a claim on her most intimate part. As his fingers slid beneath the waistband of her panties, she released another moan when his hand came into contact with her womanly folds. They were moist and she could feel the way his fingertips were spreading her juices all over it before he dipped a finger inside her.

The moment he touched her there, she pulled her mouth away from his to throw back her head in one deep moan. But he didn't let her mouth stay free for long. He recaptured it as his fingers caressed her insides in a way that almost made her weep, while his mouth continued to ply her with hungry kisses.

Suddenly she felt a sensation that started at her midsection and then spread throughout her body like tentacles of fire, building tension and strains of sensuous pressure in its wake. Her body instinctively pushed against his hand just as something within her snapped and then exploded, sending emotions, awareness and all kinds of feeling shooting all through her, flooding her with ecstasy.

Although this was the first time she'd ever experienced anything like it, she knew what it was. Callum had brought her to her first earthshaking and shattering climax. She'd heard about them and read about them, but had never experienced one before. Now she understood what it felt like to respond without limitations to a man.

When the feelings intensified, she pulled her mouth from his, closed her eyes and let out a deep piercing scream, unable to hold it back.

"That's it. Come for me, baby," he slurred thickly against her mouth before taking it again with a deep erotic thrust of his tongue.

And he kept kissing her in this devouring way of his until she felt deliciously sated and her body ceased its trembling. He finally released her mouth, but not before his tongue gave her lips a few parting licks. It was then that she opened her eyes, feeling completely drained but totally satisfied.

He held her gaze and she wondered what he was thinking. Had their business relationship been compromised? After all, he was her client and she had never been involved with a client before. And whether she'd planned it or not, they were involved. Just knowing there were more kisses where that one came from sent shivers of pleasure down her spine.

Better yet, if he could deliver this kind of pleasure to her mouth, she could just imagine what else he could do to other parts of her body, like her breasts, stomach, the area between her legs. The man possessed one hell of a dynamic tongue and he certainly knew how to use it.

Heat filled her face from those thoughts and she wondered if he saw it. At least he had no idea what she was thinking. Or did he? He hadn't said anything yet. He was just staring at her and licking his lips. She felt she should say something, but at the moment she was speechless. She'd just had her very first orgasm and she still had her clothes on. Amazing.

Callum's nostrils flared from the scent of a woman who'd been pleasured in the most primitive way. He would love to strip her naked and taste the dewy essence of her. Brand his tongue with her intimate juices, lap her up the way he'd dreamed of doing more times than he could count.

She was staring at him as if she was still trying to figure out why and how this thing had happened. He would allow her time to do that, but what he wouldn't tolerate was her thinking that what they'd shared was wrong, because it wasn't. He would not accept any regrets.

The one thing he'd taken note of with his fingers

was that she was extremely tight. With most men that would send up a red flag, but not him because her sexual experience, or lack thereof, didn't matter. However, if she hadn't been made love to before, he wanted to know it.

He opened his mouth to ask her, but she spoke before he could do so. "We should not have done that, Callum."

She could say that? While his hand was still inside of her? Maybe she had forgotten where his fingers were because they weren't moving. He flexed them, and when she immediately sucked in a deep breath as her gaze darkened with desire, he knew he'd succeeded in reminding her.

And while she watched, he slid his hand from inside of her and moments later he brought it to his lips and licked every finger that had been inside her. He then raked one finger across her lips before leaning down and tracing with his tongue where his finger had touched her mouth before saying, "With that I have to disagree." He spoke in a voice so throaty he barely recognized it as his own.

Her taste sent even more desire shooting through him. "Why do you feel that way, Gemma?"

He saw her throat move when she swallowed with her eyes still latched on his. "You're my client."

"Yes. And I just kissed you. One has nothing to do with the other. I hired you because I know you will do a good job. I just kissed you because—"

"I asked you to?"

He shook his head. "No, because I wanted to and because you wanted me to do it, too."

She nodded. "Yes," she said softly. "I wanted you to."

"Then there's no place for regrets and our attraction to each other has nothing to do with your decorating my home, so you can kill that idea here and now."

She didn't say anything for a moment and then she asked, "What about me being Ramsey's sister? Does that mean anything to you?"

A smile skidded across his lips. "I consider myself one of Ramsey's closest friends. Does that mean anything to you?"

She nervously nibbled on her bottom lip. "Yes. He will probably have a fit if he ever finds out we're attracted to each other."

"You think so?"

"Yes," she said promptly, without thinking much about his question. "Don't you?"

"No. Your brother is a fair man who recognizes you as the adult you are."

She rolled her eyes. "Are we talking about the same Ramsey Westmoreland?"

He couldn't help but grin. "Yes, we're talking about the same Ramsey Westmoreland. My best friend and your brother. You will always be one of his younger sisters, especially since he had a hand in raising you. Ramsey will always feel that he has a vested interest in your happiness and will always play the role of your protector, and understandably so. However, that doesn't mean he doesn't recognize that you're old enough to make your own decisions about your life."

She didn't say anything and he knew she was thinking hard about what he'd said. To reinforce the meaning of his words, he added. "Besides, Ramsey knows I would never take advantage of you, Gemma. I am not that kind of guy. I ask before I take. But remember, you always have the right to say no." A part of him hoped she would never say no to any direction their attraction might lead.

"I need to think about this some more, Callum."

He smiled. "Okay. That's fine. Now it's time for us to go inside."

He moved to open the door and she reached out and touched his hand. "And you won't try kissing me again?"

He reached out and pushed a strand of hair away from her face. "No, not unless you ask me to or give me an indication that's what you want me to do. But be forewarned, Gemma. If you ask, then I will deliver because I intend to be the man who will give you everything you want."

He then got out of the car and strolled to the other side to open the door for her.

He intended to being the man who gave her everything she wanted? A puzzled Gemma walked beside Callum toward his front door. When had he decided that? Before the kiss, during the kiss or after the kiss?

She shook her head. It definitely hadn't been before. Granted, they'd come close to kissing on the plane, but that had been the heat of the moment, due to an attraction that had begun sizzling below the surface. But that attraction didn't start until… When?

She pulled in a deep breath, really not certain. She'd always noticed him as a man from afar, but only in a complimentary way, since she'd assumed that he was taken. But she would be the first to admit that once he'd told her he wasn't, she'd begun seeing him in a whole different light. But she'd been realistic enough to know that, given the ten-year difference in their ages and the fact he was Ramsey's best friend, chances were that even if she was interested in him there was no way he would reciprocate that interest.

Or had it been during the kiss, when he had shown her just what a real kiss was like? Had he detected that this was her first real kiss? She'd tried following his lead, but when that lead began taking her so many different places and had made her feel a multitude of emotions and sensations she hadn't been used to, she just gave up following and let him take complete control. She had not been disappointed.

Her first orgasm had left every cell in her body feeling strung from one end to the other. She wondered just how many women could be kissed into an orgasm? She wondered how it would be if she and Callum actually made love. The pleasure just might kill her.

But then, he might have decided that he was the man to give her whatever she wanted after the kiss, when she was trying to regain control of her senses. Did he see her as a novelty? Did he want to rid her of her naiveté about certain things that happen between a man and a woman?

Evidently, he thought differently about how her oldest brother saw things. Well, she wasn't as certain as he was about Ramsey's reaction. She was well aware that she was an adult, old enough to call the shots about her own life. But with all the trouble the twins, Bane and Bailey had given everyone while growing up, she had promised herself never to cause Ramsey any unnecessary grief.

Although she would be the first to admit that she had a tendency to speak her mind whenever it suited her and she could be stubborn to a fault at times, she basically didn't cross people unless they crossed her. Those who'd known her great-grandmother—the first Gemma Westmoreland—who'd been married to Raphel, said she had inherited that attitude from her namesake. That's probably why so many family members believed there was more to the story about her great-grandfather Raphel and his bigamist ways that was yet to be uncovered. She wasn't as anxious about uncovering the truth as Dillon had been, but she knew Megan and some of her cousins were.

She stopped walking once they reached the door and Callum pulled a key from his pocket. She glanced around and saw that this particular building was set apart from the others on a secluded cul-de-sac. And it was also on a lot larger than the others, although, to her way of thinking, all of them appeared massive. "Why is your condo sitting on a street all by itself?" she asked.

"I wanted it that way for privacy."

"And they obliged you?"

He smiled. "Yes, since I bought all the other lots on this side of the complex as buffers. I didn't want to feel crowded. I'm used to a lot of space, but I liked the area because the beach is practically in my backyard."

She couldn't wait to see that, since Denver didn't have beaches. There was the Rocky Mountain Beach that included a stretch of sand but wasn't connected to an ocean like a real beach.

"Welcome to my home, Gemma."

He stood back and she stepped over the threshold at the same exact moment that he flicked a switch and the lights came on. She glanced around in awe. The interior of his home was simply beautiful and unless he had hidden decorating skills she wasn't aware of, she had to assume that he'd retained the services of a professional designer for this place, too. His colors, masculine in nature, were well-coordinated and blended together perfectly.

She moved farther into the room, taking note of everything—from the Persian rugs on the beautifully polished walnut floors, to the decorative throw pillows on the sofa, to the style of curtains and blinds that covered the massive windows. The light colors of the window treatments made each room appear larger in dimension and the banister of the spiral staircase that led to another floor gave the condo a sophisticated air.

When Callum crossed the room and lifted the blinds, she caught her breath. He hadn't lied when he'd said the beach was practically in his backyard. Even at night, thanks to the full moon overhead, she could see the beautiful waters of the Pacific Ocean.

Living away from home while attending college had taken care of any wanderlust she might have had at one time. Seeing the world had never topped her list. She was more than satisfied with the one hundred acres she had acquired on her twenty-first birthday—an inheritance for each of the Westmorelands. The section of Denver most folks considered as Westmoreland Country was all the home she'd ever known and had ever wanted. But she would have to admit that all she'd seen of Sydney so far was making it a close second.

Callum turned back to her. "So what do you think?"

Gemma smiled. "I think I'm going to love it here."

Eight

The next morning, after taking his shower, Callum dressed as he gazed out his bedroom window at the beautiful waters of the ocean. For some reason he believed it was going to be a wonderful day. He was back home and the woman he intended to share his life with was sleeping under his roof.

As he stepped into his shoes, he had to admit that he missed being back in Denver, working the ranch and spending time with the men he'd come to know over the past three years. During that time Ramsey had needed his help and they'd formed a close bond. Now Ramsey's life had moved in another direction. Ramsey was truly happy. He had a wife and a baby on the way and Callum was happy for his friend.

And more than anything he intended to find some of that same happiness for himself.

As he buttoned up his shirt, he couldn't help but think about the kiss he and Gemma had shared last night. The taste of her was still on his tongue. He'd told her that he wouldn't kiss her again until she gave the word, and he intended to do everything within his power to make sure she gave it—and soon.

The one thing he knew about Gemma was that she was stubborn. If you wanted to introduce an idea to her, you had to make her think that it had been *her* idea. Otherwise, she would balk at any suggestion you made. He had no problems doing that. When he put his seduction plan into motion, he would do it in such a way that she would think she was seducing him.

The thought of such a thing—her seducing him—had his manhood flexing. Although his feelings for Gemma were more than sexual, he couldn't help those nightly dreams that had plagued him since first meeting her. He'd seen her stripped bare—in his dreams. He'd tasted every inch of her body—in his dreams. And in his dreams he'd constantly asked what she wanted. What she needed from him to prove that she was his woman in every way.

Last night after he'd shown her the guestroom she would be using and had brought in their luggage, she had told him she was still suffering from jet lag and planned to retire early. She had quickly moved into her bedroom and had been sequestered there ever since. That was fine. In time she would find out that, when it came to him, she could run but she most certainly couldn't hide.

He would let her try to deny this thing that was developing between them, but she would discover soon enough that he was her man.

But what he wanted and needed right now was another kiss. He smiled, thinking his job was to make sure she felt that she needed another kiss as well. And as he walked out of his bedroom he placed getting another kiss at the top of his agenda.

Gemma stood in her bare feet in front of the window in Callum's kitchen as she gazed out at the beach. The view was simply amazing. She'd never seen anything like it.

One year while in college, during spring break weekend, she and a few friends had driven from Nebraska to Florida to spend the weekend on the beach in Pensacola. There she had seen a real beach with miles and miles of the purest blue-green waters. She was convinced that the Pacific Ocean was even more breathtaking and she'd come miles and miles away from home to see it.

Home.

Although she did miss home, she considered being in Australia an adventure as well as a job. Because of the difference in time zones, when she'd retired last night, she hadn't made any calls, but she intended to try to do so today. Megan was keeping tabs on the bank situation involving Niecee. With the money Callum had advanced her, her bank account was in pretty good shape, with more than enough funds to cover her debts. But she had no intention of letting Niecee get away with what she'd done. She had yet to tell anyone else in the family, other than Megan and Bailey, about the incident and planned on keeping things that way until the funds had been recovered and were back in her bank account.

She took another sip of her coffee, thinking about the kiss she and Callum had shared last night. Okay, she would admit it had been more than off the chain and the climax was simply shocking. Just the thought gave her sensuous shivers and was making her body tingle all over. What Callum had done with his tongue in her mouth and his fingers between her legs made her blush.

It had been hard getting to sleep. More than once she had dreamed of his tongue seeking hers and now that she was fully aware of what he could do with that tongue and those fingers, she wanted more.

She drew in a deep breath, thinking there was no way she would ask for a repeat performance. She could now stake a claim to knowing firsthand what an orgasm was about with her virginity still intact. Imagine that.

She couldn't imagine it when part of her dream last night dwelled on Callum making love to her and taking away her innocence, something she'd never thought of sharing with another man. The thought of being twenty-four and a virgin had never bothered her. What bothered her was knowing that there was a lot more pleasure out there that she was missing out on. Pleasure she was more than certain Callum could deliver, with or without a silver platter.

All she had to do was tell him what she wanted.

"Good morning, Gemma."

She turned around quickly, surprised that she had managed to keep from spilling her coffee. She hadn't heard Callum come down the stairs. In fact, she hadn't heard him moving around upstairs. And now he stood in the middle of his kitchen, dressed in a way she'd never seen before.

He was wearing an expensive-looking gray suit. Somehow he had gone from being a sheep-ranch manager to a well-groomed, sophisticated and suave businessman. But then the chestnut-brown hair flowing around his shoulders gave him a sort of rakish look. She wasn't sure what to make of the change and just which Callum Austell she most preferred.

"Good morning, Callum," she heard herself say, trying not to get lost in the depths of his green eyes. "You're already dressed and I'm not." She glanced down at herself. In addition to not wearing shoes, she had slipped into one of those cutesy sundresses Bailey had given as a gift for her birthday.

"No problem. The house isn't going anywhere. It will be there when you're ready to see it. I thought I'd go into the office today and let everyone know that I'm back for a while."

She lifted a brow. "The office?"

"Yes, Le'Claire Developers. It's a land development company similar to Blue Ridge Land Management. But also under the umbrella of Le'Claire are several smaller sheep ranches on the same scale as Ramsey's."

"And you are…"

"The CEO of Le'Claire," he said.

"You named it after your mother?"

He chuckled. "No, my father named it after my mother. When we all turned twenty-one, according to the terms of a trust my great-grandfather established, all four of us were set up in our own businesses. Morris, being the firstborn, will inherit the sheep farms that have been in the Austell family for generations as well as stock in all the businesses his siblings control. Colin is CEO of the chain of hotels my family owns. The one we stayed in the other night is one of them. Le'Shaunda received a slew of supermarket chains, and I was given a land development company and several small sheep ranches. Although I'm CEO, I have a staff capable of running things in my absence."

Gemma nodded, taking all this in. Bailey had tried telling her and Megan that she'd heard that Callum was loaded in his own right, but she really hadn't believed her. Why would a man as wealthy as Bailey claimed Callum was settle for being the manager of someone else's sheep ranch? Granted, he and Ramsey were close, but she couldn't see them being *so* close that Callum would give up a life of wealth and luxury for three years to live in a small cabin on her brother's property.

"Why did you do it?" she heard herself asking.

"Why did I do what?"

"It's obvious that you have money, so why would you give all this up for three years and work as the manager of my brother's sheep ranch?"

This, Callum thought, would be the perfect time to sit Gemma down and explain things to her, letting her know the reason he'd hung around Denver for three years. But he had a feeling just like when his father had tried explaining to his mother about her being his soul mate and it hadn't gone over well, it wouldn't go over well with Gemma, either.

According to Todd Austell, trying to convince Le'Claire Richards it had been love at first sight was the hardest thing he ever had to do. In fact, she figured he wanted to marry her to rebel against his parents trying to pick out a wife for him and not because he was truly in love with her.

Callum was sure that over the years his mother had pretty much kissed that notion goodbye, because there wasn't a single day that passed when his father didn't show his mother how much he loved her. Maybe that's why it came so easily to Callum to admit that he loved a woman. His father was a great role model.

But still, when it came to an Austell falling in love, Callum had a feeling that Gemma would be just as skeptical as his mother had been. So there was no way he could tell her the full truth of why he had spent three years practically right in her backyard.

"I needed to get away from my family for a while," he heard himself saying, which really wasn't a lie. He had been wild and reckless in his younger years, and returning home from college hadn't made things any better. The death of his grandfather had.

He had loved the old man dearly and he would have to say that his grandfather had spoiled him rotten. With the old man gone, there was no one to make excuses for him, no one to get him out of the scrapes he got into and no one who would listen to whatever tale he decided to fabricate. His father had decided that the only way to make him stand on his own was to make him work for it. So he had.

He had worked on his parents' ranch for a full year, right alongside the other ranch hands, to prove his worth. It had only been after he'd succeeded in doing that that his father had given him Le'Claire to run. But by then Callum had decided he much preferred a ranch-hand bunk to a glamorous thirty-floor high rise overlooking the harbor. So he had hired the best management team money could buy to run his corporation while he returned to work on his parents' ranch. That's when he'd met Ramsey and the two had quickly become fast friends.

"I understand," said Gemma, cutting into his thoughts.

He lifted a brow. He had expected her to question him further. "You do?"

"Yes. That's why Bane left home to join the Navy. He needed his space from us for a while. He needed to find himself."

Brisbane was her cousin Dillon's baby brother. From what Callum had heard, Bane had been only eight when his parents had been killed. He had grieved for them in a different way than the others, by fighting to get the attention he craved. When he'd graduated from high school, he had refused to go to college. After numerous brushes with the law and butting heads with the parents of a young lady who didn't want him to be a part of their daughter's life, Dillon had convinced Bane to get his life together. Everyone was hoping the military would eventually make a man of him.

Callum decided that he didn't want to dig himself in any deeper than he'd be able to pull himself out of when he finally admitted the truth to Gemma. "Would you like to go into the office with me for a while today? Who knows? You might be able to offer me a few decorating suggestions for there as well."

Her face lit up and he thought at that moment, she

could decorate every single thing he owned if it would get him that smile.

"You'd give me that opportunity?"

He held back from saying, *I'll give you every single thing you want, Gemma Westmoreland*. "Yes, but only if it's within my budget," he said instead.

She threw her head back and laughed, and the hair that went flying around her shoulders made his body hard. "We'll see if we can work something out," she said, moving toward the stairs. "It won't take long for me to dress. I promise."

"Take your time," he said to her fleeting back. He peeped around the corner and caught a glimpse of long, shapely legs when she lifted the hem of her outfit to rush up the stairs. His body suddenly got harder with a raw, primitive need.

He went over to the counter to pour a cup of the coffee she'd prepared, thinking he hadn't gotten that kiss yet, but he was determined to charm it out of her at some point today.

"Welcome back, Mr. Austell."

"Thanks, Lorna. Is everyone here?" Callum asked the older woman sitting behind the huge desk.

"Yes, sir. They are here and ready for today's meeting."

"Good. I'd like you to meet Gemma Westmoreland, one of my business associates. Gemma this is Lorna Guyton."

The woman switched her smile over to Gemma, who was standing by Callum's side. "Nice meeting you, Ms. Westmoreland," the woman said, offering Gemma her hand.

"Same here, Ms. Guyton." Gemma couldn't help but be pleased with the way Callum had introduced her. Saying she was a business associate sounded a lot better than saying she was merely the woman decorating one of his homes.

She glanced around, taking mental note of the layout of this particular floor of the Le'Claire Building. When they had pulled into the parking garage, she had definitely been impressed with the thirty-floor skyscraper. So far, the only thing she thought she would change with respect to the interior design, if given the chance, was the selection of paintings on the various walls.

"You can announce us to the team, Lorna," Callum said, and placing his hand on Gemma's arm, he led her toward the huge conference room.

Gemma had caught the word *us* the moment Callum touched her arm and wasn't sure which had her head suddenly spinning more—him including her in his business meeting or the way her body reacted to his touch.

She had assumed that since he would be talking business he would want her to wait in the reception area near Lorna's desk. But the fact that he had included her sent a degree of pleasure up her spine and filled her with an unreasonable degree of importance.

Now if she could just stop the flutters from going off in her stomach with the feel of his hand on her arm. But then she'd been getting all kinds of sensations—more so than ever—since they had kissed. When he'd walked into the kitchen this morning looking like he should be on the cover of *GQ* magazine, a rush of blood had shot to her head and it was probably still there. She'd had to sit beside him in the car and draw in his scent with every breath she took. And it had been hard sitting in that seat knowing what had happened last night while she'd been sitting there. On the drive over, her body had gone through some sort of battle, as if it was craving again what it once had.

"Good morning, everyone."

Gemma's thoughts were interrupted when Callum swept her into the large conference room where several people sat waiting expectantly. The men stood and the women smiled and gave her curious glances.

Callum greeted everyone by name and introduced Gemma the same way he had in speaking to Lorna. When he moved toward the chair at the head of the table, she stepped aside to take a chair in the back of the room. However, he gently tightened his grip on her arm and kept her moving toward the front with him.

He then pulled out the empty chair next to his for her to sit in. Once she had taken her seat, he took his and smiled over at her before calling the meeting to order in a deep, authoritative voice.

She couldn't help but admire how efficient he was and had to remind herself several times during the course of the business meeting that this was the same Callum who'd managed her brother's sheep farm. The same Callum who would turn feminine heads around town when he wore tight-fitting jeans over taut hips and an ultrafine tush, and sported a Western shirt over broad shoulders.

And this was the same Callum who had made her

scream with pleasure last night...in his car of all places. She glanced over at his hand, the same one whose fingers were now holding an ink pen, and remembered just where that hand had been last night and what he'd been doing with those fingers.

Suddenly, she felt very hot and figured that as long as she kept looking at his hands she would get even hotter. Over the course of the hour-long meeting, she tried to focus her attention on other things in the room like the paintings on the wall, the style of window treatments and carpeting. Given the chance, she would spruce things up in here. Unlike the other part of the office, for some reason this particular room seemed a little drab. In addition to the boring pictures hanging on the walls, the carpeting lacked any depth. She wondered what that was all about. Evidently, no one told the prior interior designer that the coloring of carpet in a business often set the mood of the employees.

"I see everyone continues to do a fantastic job for me in my absence and I appreciate that. This meeting is now adjourned," Callum said.

Gemma glanced up to see everyone getting out of their seats, filing out of the room and closing the door behind them. She turned to find Callum staring at her. "What's wrong? You seemed bored," he said.

She wondered how he'd picked up on it when his full attention should have been on the meeting he was conducting. But since he had noticed...

"Yes, but I couldn't help it. This room will bore you to tears and I have a bucket full of them." She glanced around the room. "Make that *two* buckets."

Callum threw his head back and laughed. "Do you always say whatever suits you?"

"Hey, you did ask. And yes, I usually say whatever suits me. Didn't Ramsey warn you that I have no problem giving my opinion about anything?"

"Yes, he did warn me."

She gave him a sweet smile. "Yet you hired me anyway, so, unfortunately, you're stuck with me."

Callum wanted nothing more than to lean over and plant a kiss firmly on Gemma's luscious lips and say that being stuck with her was something he looked forward to. Instead, he checked his watch. "Do you want to grab lunch before we head over to the house you'll be decorating? Then while we eat you can tell me why you have so many buckets of tears from this room."

She chuckled as she stood up. "Gladly, Mr. Austell."

Nine

"Well, here we are and I want you to tell me just what you can do with this place."

Gemma heard Callum's words, but her gaze was on the interior of a monstrosity of a house. She was totally in awe. There weren't too many homes that could render her speechless, but this mansion had before she'd stepped over the threshold. The moment he'd pulled into the driveway, she'd been overwhelmed by the architecture of it. She'd known when she'd originally seen the design of the home on paper that it was a beauty, but actually seeing it in all its grandiose splendor was truly a breathtaking moment.

"Give me the history of this house," she said, glancing around at the elegant staircase, high sculptured ceilings, exquisite crown molding and gorgeous wood floors. And for some reason she believed Callum knew it. Just from her observation of him during that morning's meeting, she'd determined that he was an astute businessman, sharp as a tack, although he preferred sporting jeans and messing with sheep to wearing a business suit and tweaking mission statements.

Over lunch she'd asked how he'd managed to keep up with his business affairs with Le'Claire while working for Ramsey. He'd explained that he had made trips back home several times when his presence had been needed on important matters. In addition, the cottage he occupied in Denver had a high-speed Internet connection, a fax machine and whatever else was needed to keep in touch with his team in Australia. And due to the difference in time zones, six in the evening in Denver was ten in the morning the next day in Sydney. He'd been able to call it a day with Ramsey around five, go home and shower and be included in a number of critical business meetings by way of conference call by seven.

"This area is historic Bellevue Hills and this house was once owned by one of the richest men in Australia. Shaun told me about it, thought I should take a look at it and make the seller an offer. I did."

"Just like that?" she asked, snapping her fingers for effect.

He met her gaze. "Just like that," he said, snapping his.

She couldn't help but laugh. "I like the way you think, Callum, because, as I said, this place is a beauty."

He shifted his gaze away from her to look back at the house. "So, it's a place where you think the average woman would want to live?"

She placed her hands on her hips. "Callum, the

average woman would die to live in a place like this. This is practically a mansion. It's fit for a queen. I know because I consider myself the average woman and I would."

"You would?"

"Of course. Now, I'm dying to take a look around and make some decorating suggestions."

"As extensive as the ones you made at lunch regarding that conference room at Le'Claire?"

"Probably," she said with a smile. "But I won't know until I go through it and take measurements." She pulled her tape measure out of her purse.

"Let's go."

He touched her arm and the moment he did so, she felt that tingling sensation that always came over her when he touched her, but now the sensations were even stronger than before.

"You okay, Gemma? You're shivering."

She drew in a deep breath as they moved from the foyer toward the rest of the house. "Yes, I'm fine," she said, refusing to look at him. *If only he knew the truth about how she was feeling.*

Callum leaned against the kitchen counter and stared over at Gemma as she stood on a ladder taking measurements of a particular window. She had long ago shed her jacket and kicked off her shoes. He looked down at her feet and thought she had pretty toes.

They had been here a couple of hours already and there were still more measurements to take. He didn't mind if he could continue to keep her up there on a ladder. Once in a while, when she moved, he'd get a glimpse of her gorgeous legs and her luscious-looking thighs.

"You're quiet."

Her observation broke into his thoughts. "What I'm doing is watching you," he said. "Having fun?"

"The best kind there is. I love doing this and I'm going to love decorating this house for you." She paused a second. "Unfortunately, I have some bad news for you."

He lifted a brow. "What bad news?"

She smiled down at him. "What I want to do in here just might break you. And, it will take me longer than the six weeks planned."

He nodded. Of course, he couldn't tell her he was counting on that very thing. "I don't have a problem with that. How is your work schedule back in Denver? Will remaining here a little longer cause problems for you?"

"No. I finished all my open projects and was about to take a vacation before bidding on others, so that's fine with me if you think you can handle a houseguest for a little while longer."

"Absolutely."

She chuckled. "You might want to think about it before you give in too easily."

"No, you might want to think about it before you decide to stay."

She glanced down at him and went perfectly still and he knew at that moment she was aware of what he was thinking. Although they had enjoyed each other's company, they had practically walked on eggshells around each other all day. After lunch he'd taken her on a tour of downtown and showed her places like the Sydney Opera House, the Royal Botanic Gardens and St. Andrew's Cathedral. And they had fed seagulls in Hyde Park before coming here. Walking beside her seemed natural, and for a while they'd held hands. Each time he had touched her she had trembled.

Did she think he wasn't aware of what those shivers meant? Did she not know what being close to her was doing to him? Could she not see the male appreciation as well as the love shining in his eyes whenever he looked at her?

Breaking eye contact, he looked at his watch. "Do you plan to measure all the windows today?"

"No, I'd planned to make this my last one for now. You will bring me back tomorrow, though, right?"

"Just ask. Whatever you want, it's yours."

"In that case, I'd like to come back to finish up this part. Then we'll need to decide on what fabrics you want," she said, moving to step down from the ladder. "The earlier the better, especially if it's something I need to backorder."

He moved away from the counter to hold the ladder steady while she descended. "Thanks," she said, when her bare feet touched the floor. He was standing right there in front of her.

"Don't mention it," he said. "Ready to go?"

"Yes."

Instead of taking her hand, he walked beside her and said nothing. He felt her looking over at him, but he refused to return her gaze. He had promised that the next time they kissed she would ask for it, but she'd failed to do that, which meant that when they got back to his place he would turn up the heat.

"You all right, Callum?"

"Yes, I'm fine. Where would you like to eat? It's dinnertime."

"Doesn't matter. I'm up for anything."

He smiled when an idea popped into his head. "Then how about me preparing dinner tonight."

She lifted a brow. "Can you cook?"

"I think I might surprise you."

She chuckled. "In that case, surprise me."

Whatever you want, it's yours.

Gemma stepped out of the Jacuzzi to dry herself while thinking that Callum had been saying that a lot lately. She wondered what he would think of her if she were to tell him that what she wanted more than anything was another dose of the pleasure he'd introduced her to last night.

Being around him most of the day had put her nerves on edge. Every time he touched her or she caught him looking at her, she felt an overwhelming need to explore the intense attraction between them. His mouth and fingers had planted a need within her that was so profound, so incredibly physical, that certain parts of her body craved his touch.

She'd heard of people being physically attracted to each other to the point of lust consuming their mind and thoughts, but such a thing had never happened to her. Until now. And why was it happening at all? What was there about Callum—other than the obvious—that had her in such a tizzy? He made her want things she'd never had before. She was tempted to go further with him than she had with any other man.

In a way she had already done that last night. There was no other man on the face of this earth who could ever lay a claim to fingering her. But Callum had done that while kissing her senseless, stirring a degree of passion within her that even now made her heart beat faster just thinking about it.

She shook her head, and tried to get a grip but failed to do so. She couldn't let go of the memories of how her body erupted in one mind-shattering orgasm. Now she knew what full-blown pleasure was about. But she knew that she hadn't even reached the tip of the iceberg and her body was aching to get pushed over that turbulent edge. The thought that there was something even more powerful, more explosive to experience sent sensual shivers through her entire being.

There were a number of reasons why she should not be thinking of indulging in an affair with Callum. And yet, there were a number of reasons why she should. She was a twenty-four-year-old virgin. To give her virginity to Callum was a plus in her book, because, in addition to being attracted to him, he would know what he was doing. She'd heard horror stories about men who didn't.

And if they were to have an affair, who would know? He wasn't the type to kiss and tell. And he didn't seem bothered by the fact that his best friend was her brother. Besides, since he would be returning to Australia to live, she didn't have the worry about running into him on a constant basis, seeing him and being reminded of what they'd done.

So what was holding her back?

She knew the answer to that question. It was the same reason she was still a virgin. She was afraid the guy she would give her virginity to would also capture her heart. And the thought of any man having her heart was something she just couldn't abide. What if he were to hurt her, break her heart the way her brothers had done to all those girls?

She nibbled on her bottom lip as she slipped into her dress to join Callum for dinner. Somehow she would have to find a way to experience pleasure without the possibility of incurring heartache. She should be able to make love with a man without getting attached. Men did it all the time. She would enter into the affair with both eyes open and not expect any more than what she got. And when it was over, her heart would still be intact. She wouldn't set herself up like those other girls who'd fancied themselves in love with a Westmoreland, only to have their hearts broken.

It should be a piece of cake. After all, Callum had told her he was waiting to meet his soul mate. So there would be no misunderstanding on either of their parts. She wasn't in love with him and he wasn't in love with her. He would get what he wanted and she would be getting what she wanted.

More of last night.

A smile of anticipation touched her lips. She mustn't appear too eager and intended to play this out for all it was worth and see how long it would last. She was inexperienced when it came to seduction, but she was a quick study.

And Callum was about to discover just how eager she was to learn new things.

Callum heard Gemma moving around upstairs. He had encouraged her to relax and take a bubble bath in the huge Jacuzzi garden tub while he prepared dinner.

Since they'd eaten a large lunch at one of the restaurants downtown near the Sydney Harbour, he decided to keep dinner simple—a salad and an Aussie meat pie.

He couldn't help but smile upon recalling her expression when she'd first seen his home, and her excitement about decorating it just the way she liked. He had gone along with every suggestion she made, and although she had teased him about the cost, he knew she was intentionally trying to keep prices low, even though he'd told her that doing so wasn't necessary.

His cell phone rang and he pulled it off his belt to answer it. "Hello."

"How are you doing, Callum?"

He smiled upon hearing his mother's voice. "I'm fine, Mom. What about you?"

"I'm wonderful. I hadn't talked to you since you were here yesterday with Gemma, and I just want you to know that I think she's a lovely girl."

"Thanks, Mom. I think so, too. I just can't wait for her to figure out she's my soul mate."

"Have patience, Callum."

He chuckled. "I'll try."

"I know Gemma is going to be tied up with decorating that house, but Shaun and I were wondering if she'll be free to do some shopping with us next Friday," his mother said. "Annette and Mira will be joining us as well."

The thought of Gemma being out of his sight for any period of time didn't sit well with him. He knew all about his mother, sister and sisters-in-law's shopping trips. They could be gone for hours. He felt like a possessive lover. A smile touched his lips. He wasn't Gemma's lover yet, but he intended to be while working diligently to become a permanent part of her life—namely, her husband.

"Callum?"

"Yes, Mom. I'm sure that's something Gemma will enjoy. She's upstairs changing for dinner. I'll have her call you."

He conversed with his mother for a little while longer before ending the call. Pouring a glass of wine, he moved to the window that looked out over the Pacific. His decision to keep this place had been an easy one. He loved the view as well as the privacy.

The house Gemma was decorating was in the suburbs, sat on eight acres of land and would provide plenty of room for the large family he wanted them to have. He took a sip of wine while his mind imagined a pregnant Gemma, her tummy round with his child.

He drew in a deep breath, thinking that if anyone would have told him five years ago that he would be here in this place and in this frame of mind, he would have been flabbergasted. His mother suggested that he have patience. He'd shown just how much patience he had for the past three years. Now it was time to make his move.

"Callum?"

The sound of her voice made him turn around. He swallowed deeply, while struggling to stay where he was, not cross the room, pull her into his arms and give her the greeting that he preferred. As usual, she looked beautiful, but there was something different about her this evening. There was a serene glow to her face that hadn't been there before. Had just two days in Australia done that to her? Hell, he hoped so. More than anything, he wanted his native land to grow on her.

"You look nice, Gemma," he heard himself saying.

"Thanks. You look nice yourself."

He glanced down at himself. He had changed out of his suit, and was now wearing jeans and a pullover shirt. She was wearing an alluring little outfit—a skirt that fell a little past her knees, a matching top and a cute pair of sandals. He looked at her and immediately thought of one word. *Sexy.* Umm, make that two words. *Super sexy.* He knew of no other woman who wore her sexuality quite the way Gemma did.

His gaze roamed the full length of her in male appreciation, admiring the perfection of her legs, ankles and calves. He had to have patience, as his mother suggested and tamp down his rising desire. But all he had to do was breathe in, take a whiff of her scent and know that would not be an easy task.

"What are you drinking?"

Her words pulled his attention from her legs back to her face. "Excuse me? I missed that."

A smile curved her lips. "I asked what you're drinking."

He held up his glass and glanced at it. "Wine. Want some?"

"Sure."

"No problem. I'll pour you a glass," he said.

"No need," she said, walking slowly toward him. He felt his pulse rate increase and his breathing get erratic with every step she took.

"I'll just share yours," she said, coming to a stop in front of him. She reached out, slid the glass from his hand and took a sip. But not before taking the tip of her tongue and running it along the entire rim of the glass.

Callum sucked in a quick breath. Did she know how intimate that gesture was? He watched as she then took a sip. "Nice, Callum. Australia's finest, I assume."

He had to swallow before answering, trying to retain control of his senses. "Yes, a friend of my father owns a winery. There's plenty where that came from. Would you like some more?"

Her smile widened. "No, thank you. But there is something that I do want," she said, taking a step closer to him.

"Is there?" he said, forcing the words out of a tight throat. "You tell me what you want and, as I said yesterday and again today, whatever you want I will deliver."

She leaned in closer and whispered. "I'm holding you to your word, Callum Austell, because I've decided that I want you."

Ten

Gemma half expected Callum to yank her down and take her right there on the living room floor. After all, she'd just stated that she wanted him, and no one would have to read between the lines to figure out what that meant. Most men would immediately act on her request, not giving her the chance to change her mind.

Instead, Callum deliberately and slowly put his glass down. His gaze locked with hers and when his hands went to her waist he moved, bringing their bodies in close contact. "And what you want, Gemma, is just what you will get."

She saw intense heat in the depths of his eyes just seconds before he lowered his mouth to hers. The moment she felt his tongue invade her mouth, she knew he would be kissing her senseless.

He didn't disappoint her.

The last time they'd kissed, he had introduced her to a range of sensations that she'd never encountered before. Sensations that started at her toes and worked their way up to the top of her head. Sensations that had lingered in her lower half, causing the area between her legs to undergo all kinds of turbulent feelings and her heart all kinds of unfamiliar emotions.

This kiss was just as deadly, even more potent than the last, and her head began swimming in passion. She felt that drowning would soon follow. Blood was rushing, fast and furiously, through her veins with every stroke of his tongue. He was lapping her up in a way that had her entire body shuddering from the inside out.

Callum had encouraged her to ask for what she wanted and was delivering in full measure. He wasn't thinking about control of any kind and neither was she. He had addressed and put to rest the only two concerns she had—his relationship with her brother and her relationship with him as a client. Last night, he'd let her know that those two things had nothing to do with this— the attraction between them—and she was satisfied with that.

And now she was getting satisfied with this—his ability to deliver a kiss that was so passionate it was nearly engulfing her in flames. He was drinking her as if she were made of the finest wine, even finer than the one he'd just consumed.

She felt the arms around her waist tighten and when he shifted their positions she felt something else, the thick hardness behind the zipper of his jeans. When she moved her hip and felt his hard muscles aligned with her curves, the denim of his jeans rubbing against her bare legs, she moaned deep in her throat.

Callum released Gemma's mouth and drew in a deep breath and her scent. She smelled of the strawberry bubble bath she had used and whatever perfume she had dabbed on her body.

He brushed kisses across her forehead, eyebrows, cheeks and temples while giving her a chance to breathe. Her mouth was so soft and responsive, and it tasted so damn delicious. The more he deepened the kiss, the more responsive she became and the more accessible she made her mouth.

His hands eased from her waist to smooth across her back before cupping her backside. He could feel every inch of her soft curves beneath the material of her skirt and top, and instinctively, he pulled her closer to the fit of him.

"Do you want more?" he whispered against her lips, tasting the corners of her mouth while moaning deep in his throat from how good she tasted.

"Yes, I want more," she said in a purr that conveyed a little catch in her breathing.

"How much more?" He needed to know. Any type of rational thought and mind control was slipping away from him big time. It wouldn't take much to strip her naked right now.

He knew for a fact that she'd rarely dated during the time he'd been in Denver. And although he wasn't sure what she did while she was in college, he had a feeling his Gemma was still a virgin. The thought of that filled him with intense pride that she would give him the honor of being her first.

"I want all you can give me, Callum," she responded in a thick slur, but the words were clear to his ears.

He sucked a quick gulp of air into his lungs. He wondered if she had any idea what she was asking for. What he could give was a whole hell of a lot. If he had his way, he would keep her on her back for days. Stay inside her until he'd gotten her pregnant more times than humanly possible.

The thought of his seed entering her womanly channel, made the head of his erection throb behind his zipper, begging for release, practically pleading for the chance to get inside her wet warmth.

"Are you on any type of birth control?" He knew that she was. He had overheard a conversation once that she'd had with Bailey and knew she'd been taking oral contraceptives to regulate her monthly cycle.

"Yes, I'm on the pill," she acknowledged. "But not because I sleep around or anything like that. In fact, I'm…"

She stopped talking in midsentence and was gazing up at him beneath her long lashes. Her eyes were wide, as if it just dawned on her what she was about to reveal. He had no intention of letting her stop talking now.

"You're what?"

He watched as she began nervously nibbling on her bottom lip and he almost groaned, tempted to replace her lip with his and do the nibbling for her.

He continued to brush kisses across her face, drinking in her taste. And when she didn't respond to his inquiry, he pulled back and looked at her. "You can tell me anything, Gemma. Anything at all."

"I don't know," she said in a somewhat shaky voice. "It might make you want to stop."

Not hardly, he thought, and knew he needed to convince her of that. "There's nothing you can tell me that's going to stop me from giving you want you want. Nothing," he said fervently.

She gazed up into his eyes and he knew she believed him. She held the intensity in his gaze when she leaned forward and whispered. "I'm still a virgin."

"Oh, Gemma," he said, filled with all the love any man could feel for a woman at that particular moment. He had suspected as much, but until she'd confessed the truth, he hadn't truly been certain. Now he was, and the thought that he would be the man who carried her over the threshold of womanhood gave him pause, had him searching for words to let her know just how he felt.

He hooked her chin with his fingers as he continued to hold her gaze. "You trust me enough with such a precious gift?"

"Yes," she said promptly without hesitation.

Filled with both extreme pleasure and profound pride, he bent his head and kissed her gently while sweeping her off her feet into his arms.

When Callum placed her on his bed and stepped back to stare at her, one look at his blatantly aroused features let Gemma know that he was going to give her just what she had asked for. Just what she wanted.

Propped up against his pillow, she drank him in from head to toe as he began removing his shoes. Something—she wasn't sure just what—made her bold enough to ask. "Will you strip for me?"

He lifted his head and looked over at her. If he was shocked by her request, he didn't show it. "Is that what you want?"

"Yes."

He smiled and nodded. "No problem."

Gemma shifted her body into a comfortable position as a smile suffused her face. "Be careful or I'll begin to think you're easy."

He shrugged broad shoulders as he began removing his shirt. "Then I guess I'll just have to prove you wrong."

She chuckled. "Oooh, I can't wait." She stared at his naked chest. He was definitely built, she thought.

He tossed his shirt aside and when his hand went to the zipper of his jeans, a heated sensation began traveling along Gemma's nerve endings. When he began lowering the zipper, she completely held her breath.

He slid the zipper halfway down and met her gaze. "Something I need to confess before I go any further."

Her breath felt choppy. "What?"

"I dreamed about you last night."

Gemma smiled, pleased with his confession. "I have a confession of my own." He lifted his brows. "I dreamed about you, too. But, then, I think it was to be expected after last night."

He went back to slowly easing his zipper down. "You could have come to my bedroom. I would not have minded."

"I wasn't ready."

He didn't move as he held her gaze. "And now?"

She grinned. "And now I'm a lady-in-waiting."

He threw his head back and laughed as he began

sliding his pants down his legs. She scooted to the edge of the bed to watch, fascinated when he stood before her wearing a skimpy pair of black briefs. He had muscular thighs and a nice pair of hairy legs. The way the briefs fit his body had her shuddering when she should have been blushing.

All her senses suddenly felt hot-wired, her heart began thumping like crazy in her chest and a tingling sensation traveled up her nerve endings. She felt no shame in staring at him. The only thing she could think of at that moment was that *her* Aussie was incredibly sexy.

Her Aussie?

She couldn't believe her mind had conjured up such a thought. He wasn't hers and she wasn't his. At least not in *that* way. But tonight, she conceded, and whenever they made love, just for that moment, they would belong to each other in every way.

"Should I continue?"

She licked her lips in anticipation. "I might hurt you if you don't."

He chuckled as he slid his hands into the waistband of his briefs and slowly began easing them down his legs. "Oh my…" She could barely get the words past her throat.

Her breasts felt achy as she stared at that part of his anatomy, which seemed to get larger right before her eyes. She caught a lip between her teeth and tried not to clamp down too hard. But he had to be, without a doubt, in addition to being totally aroused and powerfully male, the most beautiful man she'd ever seen. And he stood there, with his legs braced apart, his hands on his hips and with a mass of hair flowing around his face, fully exposed to her. This was a man who could make women drool. A man who would get a second look whenever he entered a room, no matter what he was wearing. A man whose voice alone could make woman want to forget about being a good girl and just enjoy being bad.

She continued to stare, unable to do anything else, as he approached the bed. She moved into a sitting position to avoid being at eye level with his erection.

Gemma couldn't help wondering what his next move would be. Did he expect her to return the favor and strip for him? When he reached the edge of the bed, she tilted her head back and met his gaze. "My turn?"

He smiled. "Yes, but I want to do things differently."

She lifted a confused brow. "Differently?"

"Yes, instead of you stripping yourself, I want to do it."

She swallowed, not sure she understood. "You want to take my clothes off?"

He shook his head as a sexy smile touched his lips. "No, I want to strip your clothes off you."

And then he reached out and ripped off her blouse.

The surprised look on her face was priceless. Callum tossed her torn blouse across the room. And now his gaze was fixed on her chest and her blue satin push-up bra. Fascinated, he thought she looked sexy as hell.

"You owe me for that," she said when she found her voice.

"And I'll pay up," he responded as he leaned forward to release the front clasp and then eased the straps down her shoulders, freeing what he thought were perfect twin mounds with mouth-watering dark nipples.

His hand trembled when he touched them, fondled them between his eager fingers, while watching her watch him, and seeing how her eyes darkened, and how her breath came out in a husky moan.

"Hold those naughty thoughts, Gemma," he whispered when he released her and reached down to remove her sandals, rubbing his hands over her calves and ankles, while thinking her skin felt warm, almost feverish.

"Why do women torture their feet with these things?" His voice was deep and husky. He dropped the shoes by the bed.

"Because we know men like you enjoy seeing us in them."

He continued to rub her feet when he smiled. "I like seeing *you* in them. But then I like seeing you out of them, too."

His hand left her feet and began inching up her leg, past her knee to her thigh. But just for a second. His hand left her thigh and shifted over to the buttons on her skirt and with one tug sent them flying. She lifted her hips when he began pulling the skirt from her body and when she lay before him wearing nothing but a pair of skimpy blue panties, he felt blood rush straight to his heads. Both of them.

But it was the one that decided at that moment to almost double in size that commanded his attention. Without saying a word, he slowly began easing her panties down her thighs and her luscious scent began playing havoc with his nostrils as he did so.

He tossed her panties aside and his hands eased back

between her legs, seeing what he'd touched last night and watching once again as her pupils began dilating with pleasure.

And to make sure she got the full Callum Austell effect, he bent his head toward her chest, captured a nipple in his mouth and began sucking on it.

"Callum!"

"Umm?" He released that nipple only to move to the other one, licking the dark area before easing the tip between his lips and sucking on it as he'd done to the other one. He liked her taste and definitely liked the sounds she was making.

Moments later he began inching lower down her body and when his mouth came to her stomach, he traced a wet path all over it.

"Callum."

"I'm right here. You still sure you want me?" His fingers softly flicked across her womanly folds while he continued to lick her stomach.

"Oh, yes."

"Are there any limitations?" he asked.

"No."

"Sure?"

"Positive."

He took her at her word and moved his mouth lower. Her eyes began closing when he lifted her hips and wrapped her legs around his neck, lowered his head and pressed his open mouth to her feminine core.

Pleasure crashed over Gemma and she bit down to keep from screaming. Callum's tongue inside her was driving her crazy, and pushing her over the edge in a way she'd never been pushed before. Her body seemed to fragment into several pieces and each of those sections was being tortured by a warm, wet and aggressive tongue that was stroking her into a stupor.

Her hands grabbed tight to the bedspread as her legs were nudged further apart when his mouth burrowed further between her thighs and his tongue seem to delve inside her deeper.

She continued to groan in pleasure, not sure she would be able to stop moaning even when he ceased doing this to her. She released a deep moan when the pressure of his mouth on her was too much, and the erotic waves she was drowning in gave her little hope for a rescue.

And then, just like the night before, she felt her body jackknife into an orgasm that had her screaming. She was grateful for the privacy afforded by the seclusion of Callum's condo.

"Gemma."

Callum's deep Australian voice flowed through her mind as her body shuddered nearly uncontrollably. It had taken her twenty-four years to share this kind of intimacy with a man and it was well worth the wait.

"Open your eyes. I want you to be looking at me the moment I make you mine."

She lifted what seemed like heavy lids and saw that he was over her, his body positioned between her legs, and her hips were cupped in the palms of his hands. She pushed the thought out of her mind that she would never truly be his, and what he'd said was just a figure of speech, words just for the moment, and she understood because at this moment she wanted to be his.

As she gazed up into his eyes, something stirred

deep in her chest around her heart and she forced the feeling back, refusing to allow it to gain purchase there, rebuffing the very notion and repudiating the very idea. This was about lust, not love. He knew it and she knew it as well. There was nothing surprising about the way her body was responding to him; the way he seemed to be able to strum her senses the same way a musician strummed his guitar.

And then she felt him, felt the way his engorged erection was pressed against her femininity and she kept her gaze locked with his when she felt him make an attempt to slide into her. It wasn't easy. He was trying to stretch her and it didn't seem to be working. Sweat popped on his brow and she reached up and wiped his forehead with the back of her hand.

He saw her flinch in pain and he went still. "Do you want me to stop?"

She shook her head from side to side. "No. I want you to make it happen, and you said you'll give me what I want."

"Brat," he said. When she chuckled, he thrust forward. When she cried out he leaned in and captured her lips.

You truly belong to me now and I love you, Callum wanted to say, but knew that he couldn't. Instead, after her body had adjusted to his, he began moving. Every stroke into her body was a sign of his love whether she knew it or not. One day when she could accept it, she would know and he would gladly tell her everything.

He needed to kiss her, join his mouth to hers the same way their bodies were joined. So he leaned close and captured her mouth, kissing her thoroughly and hungrily, and with a passion he felt through every cell in his body.

When she instinctively began milking his erection, he deepened the kiss.

And when he felt her body explode, which triggered his to do likewise, he pulled his mouth from hers to throw his head back to scream her name. *Her name*. No other woman's name but hers, while he continued to thrust in and out of her.

His body had ached for this for so long, his body had ached for her. And as a climax continued to rip through them, he knew that, no matter what, Gemma Westmoreland was what he needed in his life and there was no way he would ever give her up.

Eleven

Sunlight flitting across her face made Gemma open her eyes and she immediately felt the hard muscular body sleeping beside her. Callum's leg was thrown over hers and his arms were wrapped around her middle. They were both naked—that was a given—and the even sound of his breathing meant he was still asleep.

The man was amazing. He had made love to her in a way that made her first time with a man so very special. He'd also fed her last night the tasty meal he'd prepared, surprising her and proving that he was just as hot in the kitchen as he was in the bedroom.

She drew in a deep breath, wondering which part of her was sorer, the area between her legs or her breasts. Callum had given special attention to both areas through most of the night. But with a tenderness that touched her deeply, he had paused to prepare a warm, soothing soak for her in his huge bathtub. He hadn't made love to her since then. They'd eaten a late dinner, and returning to bed, he had cuddled her in his arms, close to his warm, masculine body. His hands had caressed her all over, gently stroking her to sleep.

And now she was awake and very much aware of everything they'd done the night before. Everything she'd asked him for, he had delivered. Even when he had wanted to stop because last night was her first time, she had wanted to experience more pleasure and he had ended up making it happen, giving her what she wanted. And although her body felt sore and battered today, a part of her felt that last night had truly been worth it.

Deciding to get a little more sleep, she closed her eyes and immediately saw visions of them together. But it wasn't a recent image. She looked older and so did he and there were kids around. Whose kids were they? Certainly not theirs. Otherwise that would mean…

Her eyes sprang open, refusing to let such an apparition enter her mind. She would be the first to admit that what they'd shared last night had overwhelmed her, and for a moment she'd come close to challenging everything she believed about relationships between men and women. But the last thing she needed to do was get offtrack. Last night was what it was—no more, no less. It was about a curious, inexperienced woman and a horny, experienced man. And both had gotten satisfied to the nth degree. They had both gotten what they wanted.

"You're awake?"

Callum's voice sent sensations running across her skin. "Who wants to know?"

"The man who made love to you last night."

She shifted her body, turned to face him and immediately wished she hadn't. Fully awake he was sexy as sin. A half asleep Callum, with a stubble chin, drowsy eyes and long eyelashes, could make you come just looking at him.

"You're the one who did that to me last night, aren't you?"

A smile curved his lips. "I'm the one who plans to do that to you every night."

She chuckled, knowing he only meant every night she remained in Australia. She was certain he knew that when they returned to Denver things would be different. Although she had her own little place, he would not be making late-night booty calls on her Westmoreland property.

"You think you have the stamina to do it every night?"

"Don't you?"

She had to admit that the man's staying power was truly phenomenal. But she figured, in time, when she got the hang of it, she would be able to handle him. "Yes, I do."

She then reached out and rubbed a hand across his chin. "You need a shave."

He chuckled. "Do I?"

"Yes." Then she grabbed a lock of his hair. "And…"

"Don't go there. I get my hair trimmed, never cut."

She smiled. "That must be an Austell thing, since I see your father and brothers evidently feel the same way. Don't be surprised if I start calling you Samson."

"And I'll start calling you Delilah, the temptress."

She couldn't help but laugh. "I wouldn't know how to tempt a man."

"But you know how to tempt me."

"Do I?"

"Yes, but don't get any ideas," he said. "Last night you made me promise to get you to your new office by ten o'clock."

Yes, she had made him promise that. He'd told her she could set up shop in the study of the house. He would have a phone installed as well as a fax machine and a computer with a high-speed Internet connection. The sooner she could get the materials she needed ordered, the quicker she could return to Denver. For some reason, the thought of returning home tugged at her heart. This was her third day here and she already loved this place.

"You do want to be on the job by ten, right?"

A smile touched her lips. "Yes, I do. Have you decided when and if you're returning to Denver?" She just had to know.

"Yes, I plan to return with you and will probably stay until after Ramsey and Chloe's baby is born to help out on the ranch. When things get pretty much back to normal for Ramsey, then I'll leave Denver for good and return here."

She began nibbling on her bottom lip. This was September, and Chloe was due to deliver in November, which meant Callum would be leaving Denver a few months after that. Chances were there would be no Callum Austell in Denver come spring.

"Umm, let me do that."

She lifted her gaze to his eyes when he interrupted her thoughts. "Let you do what?"

"This."

He leaned closer and began gently nibbling on her lips, then licking her mouth from corner to corner. When her lips parted on a breathless sigh, he entered her mouth to taste her fully. The kiss grew deeper, hotter and moments later, when he pulled his mouth away, he placed his fingers to her lips to stop the request he knew she was about to make.

"Your body doesn't need me that way, Gemma. It needs an adjustment period," he whispered against her lips.

She nodded. "But later?"

His lips curved in a wicked smile. "Yes, later."

Callum was vaguely aware of the information the foreman of one of his sheep ranches was giving to him. The report was good, which he knew it would be. During the time he'd been in Denver, he'd pretty much kept up with things here as well as with Le'Claire. He'd learned early how to multitask.

And he smiled, thinking how well he'd multi-tasked last night. There hadn't been one single part of Gemma he hadn't wanted to devour—and all at the same time. He'd been greedy, and so had she. His woman had more passion in her body than she knew what to do with, and he was more than willing to school her in all the possibilities. But he also knew that he had to be careful. He didn't want her to start thinking that what was between them was more lust than love. His goal was to woo her every chance he got, which is why he'd hung up with the florist a few moments ago.

"So as you can see, Mr. Austell, everything is as it should be."

He smiled at the man who'd been talking for the past ten minutes, going over his sheep-herding records. "I figured they would be. I appreciate the job you and your men have done in my absence, Richard."

A huge grin covered the man's face. "We appreciate working for the Austells."

Richard Vinson and his family had worked on an Austell sheep ranch for generations. In fact, upon Callum's grandfather's death, Jack Austell had deeded over five hundred acres of land to the Vinson family in recognition of their loyalty, devotion and hard work.

A few minutes later, Callum was headed back to his car when his phone rang. A quick check showed it was a call from the States, namely Derringer Westmoreland. "Yes, Derringer?"

"Just calling to see if you've given any more thought to becoming a silent partner in our horse-breeding venture?"

Durango Westmoreland, part of those Atlanta Westmorelands, had teamed up with a childhood friend and cousin-in-law named McKinnon Quinn, and bought a very successful horse-breeding and -training operation in Montana. They had invited their cousins, Zane, Derringer and Jason, to become part of their outfit as Colorado partners. Callum, Ramsey and Dillon had expressed an interest in becoming silent partners. "Yes. I'm impressed with all I've heard about it, so count me in."

"Boy, you're easy," Derringer teased.

His words made Callum think about Gemma. She had said the same thing to him last night, but during the course of the night he'd shown her just how wrong she was. "Hey, what can I say? Are you behaving yourself?"

Derringer laughed. "Hey, now what can I say? And speaking of behaving, how is that sister of mine? She hasn't driven you crazy yet?"

Callum smiled. Gemma had driven him crazy but in a way he'd rather not go into with her brother. "Gemma is doing a great job decorating my place."

"Well, watch your wallet. I heard her prices can sometimes get out of sight."

"Thanks for the warning."

He talked to Derringer a few moments longer before ending the call. After he married Gemma, Ramsey, Zane, Derringer, the twins, Megan and Bailey would become his in-laws, and those other Westmorelands, including Dillon, his cousins-in-law. Hell, he didn't want to think about all those other Westmorelands, the ones from Atlanta that Ramsey and his siblings and cousins were just beginning to get to know. It didn't take the Denver Westmorelands and the Atlanta Westmorelands long to begin meshing as if they'd had a close relationship all their lives.

Callum's father had been an only child and so had his father before him. Todd Austell probably would have been content having one child, but Le'Claire had had a say in that. His father had known that marrying the American beauty meant fathering at least three children. Callum chuckled, remembering that, according to his father, his birth had been a surprise. Todd had assumed his daddy days were over, but Le'Claire had had other ideas about that, and Todd had decided to give his wife whatever she wanted. Callum was using that same approach with Gemma. Whatever this particular Westmoreland wanted is what she would get.

After Callum snapped his seat belt in place, he checked his watch. It was a little past three and he would be picking Gemma up around five. He'd wanted to take her to lunch, but she'd declined, saying she had a lot of orders to place if he wanted the house fully decorated and ready for him to move in by November.

He really didn't care if he was in that house, still living in his condo on the beach or back in Denver. All that mattered to him was that Gemma was with him—wherever he was. And as he turned the ignition to his car, he knew that making that happen was still his top priority.

"Will there be anything else, Ms. Westmoreland?"

Gemma glanced up at the older woman Callum had introduced her to that morning, Kathleen Morgan. "No, Kathleen. That's it. Thanks for all you did today."

The woman waved off her words. "I didn't do anything but make a lot of phone calls to place those orders. I can just imagine how this place is going to look when you finish with it. I think Mr. Austell's decision to blend European and Western styles will be simply beautiful. One day this house will be a showplace for Mr. Austell and his future wife. Good bye."

"Goodbye." Gemma tried letting the woman's words pass, but couldn't. The thought of Callum sharing this house with a woman—one he would be married to—bothered her.

She tossed her pencil on the desk and glanced over at the flowers that had been delivered not long after he'd dropped her off here. A dozen red roses. Why had he sent them? The card that accompanied them only had his signature. They were simply beautiful, and the fragrance suffused her office.

Her office.

And that was another mystery. She had assumed she would have an empty room on the main floor of the house with a table and just the bare essentials to operate as a temporary place to order materials and supplies. But when she'd stepped through the door with Callum at her back, she had seen that the empty room had been transformed into a work place, equipped with everything imaginable, including a live administrative assistant.

She pushed her chair back and walked across the room to the vase of flowers she'd placed on a table in front of a window. That way she could pause while working to glance over at them and appreciate their beauty. Unfortunately, seeing them also made her think of the man who'd sent them.

She threw her head back in frustration. She had to stop thinking of Callum and start concentrating on the job he'd hired her to do. Not only had he hired her, he had brought her all the way from Denver to handle her business.

But still, today she'd found herself remembering last night and this morning. True to his word, he had not made love to her again, but he had held her, tasted her lips and given her pleasure another way. Namely with his mouth. He had soothed her body and brought it pleasure at the same time. Amazing.

She turned when her cell phone rang and quickly crossed the room to pick it up. It was her sister, Megan. "Megan, how are you doing?" She missed her sisters.

"I'm fine. I have Bailey here with me and she says hello. We miss you."

"And I miss you both, too," she said honestly. "What time is it there?" She placed her cell phone on speaker to put away the files spread all over her desk.

"Close to ten on Monday night. It's Tuesday there already, right?"

"Yes, Tuesday afternoon around four. Today was my first day on the job. Callum set a room up at the house for me to use as an office. I even have an administrative assistant. And speaking of administrative assistants, has the bank's security team contacted you about Niecee?"

"Yes, in fact I got a call yesterday. It seems she deposited the check in an account in Florida. They are working with that bank to stop payment. What's in your favor is that you acted right away. Most businesses that are the victims of embezzlement don't find out about the thefts until months later, and then it's too late to recover the funds. Niecee gave herself away when she left that note apologizing the next day. Had she been bright she would have called in sick a few days, waited for the check to clear and then confessed her sins. Now it looks like she'll be getting arrested."

Gemma let out a deep sigh. A part of her felt bad, but then what Niecee had done was wrong. The woman probably figured that because Gemma was a

Westmoreland she had the money to spare. Well, she was wrong. Dillon and Ramsey had pretty much drilled into each of them to make their own way. Yes, they'd each been given one hundred acres and a nice trust fund when they'd turned twenty-one, but making sure they used that money responsibly was up to them. So far all of them had. Luckily, Bane had turned his affairs over to Dillon to handle. Otherwise, he would probably be penniless by now.

"Well, I regret that, but I can't get over what she did. Twenty thousand dollars is not small change."

A sound made Gemma turn around and she drew in a deep breath when she saw Callum standing there, leaning in the doorway. And from the expression on his face, she knew he'd been listening to her and Megan's conversation. How dare he! She wondered if he would mention it to Ramsey.

"Megan, I'll call you back later," she said, placing her phone off speaker. "Tell everyone I said hello and give them my love."

She ended the call and placed the phone back on her desk. "You're early."

"Yes, you might say that," he said, crossing his arms across his chest. "What's this about your administrative assistant embezzling money from you?"

Gemma threw her head back, sending hair flying over her shoulders. "You were deliberately eavesdropping on my conversation."

"You placed the call on speaker and I just happened to arrive while the conversation was going on."

"Well, you could have let me know you were here."

"Yes, I could have. Now answer the question about Niecee."

"No. It's none of your business," she snapped.

He strolled into the room toward her. "That's where you're wrong. It *is* my business, on both a business and a personal level."

A frown deepened her brow. "And how do you figure that?"

He came to a stop in front of her. "First of all, on a business level, before I do business with anyone I expect the company to be financially sound. In other words, Gemma, I figured that you had enough funds in your bank account to cover the initial outlay for this decorating job."

She placed her hands on her hips. "I didn't have to worry about that since you gave me such a huge advance."

"And what if I hadn't done that? Would you have been able to take the job here?"

Gemma didn't have to think about the answer to that. "No, but—"

"No, buts, Gemma." He didn't say anything for a minute and it seemed as if he was struggling not to smile. That only fueled her anger. What did he find so amusing?

Before she could ask, he spoke. "And it's personal, Gemma, because it's you. I don't like the idea of anyone taking advantage of you. Does Ramsey know?"

Boy, that did it! "I own Designs by Gems—not Ramsey. It's my business and whatever problems crop up are *my* problems. I know I made a mistake in hiring Niecee. I see that now and I should have listened to

Ramsey and Dillon and done a background check on her, as they suggested. I didn't and I regret it. But at least I'm—"

"Handling your business." He glanced at his watch. "Ready to go?" he asked, walking away and heading for the door, turning off the light switch in the process. "There's a nice restaurant not far from here that I think you'll like."

Gemma spun around to face him. "I'm not going anywhere with you. I'm mad."

Callum flashed her a smile. "Then get over it."

Gemma was too undone…and totally confused. "I won't be getting over it."

He nodded. "Okay, let's talk about it then."

She crossed her arms over her chest. "I don't want to talk about it, because it's none of your business."

Callum threw his head back and laughed. "We're back to that again?"

Gemma glared at him. "We need to get a few things straight, Callum."

He nodded. "Yes, we do." He walked back over to her. "I've already told you why it's my business and from a business perspective you see that I'm right, don't you?"

It took her a full minute, but she finally said, "Yes, all right. I see that. I'll admit that you are right from a business perspective. That's not the way I usually operate but…"

"You were robbing Peter to pay Paul, I know. However, I don't like being Peter or Paul. Now, as far as it being personal, *you* were right."

She lifted a brow. "I was?"

"Yes. It was your business and not Ramsey's concern. I admitted it and told you that you handled it. That was the end of it," he said.

She gave herself a mental shake, trying to keep up with him. He had scolded her on one hand, but complimented her way of handling things on the other. "So you won't mention it to Ramsey?"

"No. It's not my place to do that…unless your life is in danger or something equally as dire, and it's not." He looked down at her and smiled. "As I said, from the sound of the conversation you just had with Megan, you handled this matter in an expeditious manner. By all accounts, you will be getting your money back. Kudos for you."

A smile crossed Gemma's lips. She was proud of herself. "Yes, kudos for me." Her eyes narrowed. "And just what did you find amusing earlier?"

"How quickly you can get angry just for the sake of doing so. I'd heard about your unique temperament but never experienced it before."

"Did it bother you?"

"No."

Gemma frowned, not sure how she felt about that. In a way she liked that Callum didn't run for cover when her temper exploded, as it did at times. Zane, Derringer and the twins were known to have had a plate aimed at their heads once or twice, and knew to be ready to duck if they gave her sufficient cause.

"However, I would like you to make me a promise," he said, breaking into her thoughts.

She lifted a curious brow. "What?"

"Promise that if you ever find yourself in a bind again, financial or otherwise, you'll let me know."

She rolled her eyes. "I don't need another older brother, Callum."

He smiled and his teeth flashed a bright white against his brown skin. "There's no way you can think we have anything close to a brother-sister relationship after last night. But just in case you need a little reminder..."

He pulled her into his arms, lowered his head and captured her mouth with his.

Twelve

Gemma's face blushed with anticipation as she walked into Callum's condo. Dinner was fantastic, but she liked being back here alone with him.

"Are you tired, Gemma?"

He had to be kidding. She glanced over her shoulder and gave him a wry look. He was closing the door and locking it. "What makes you think that?"

"You were kind of quiet at dinner."

She chuckled. "Not hardly. I nearly talked your ears off."

"And I nearly talked yours off, too."

She shook her head. "No, you didn't. You were sharing how your day went, and basically, I was doing the same." *While sitting there nearly drooling over you from across the table.* Now that they were alone, she wondered if she would have to tell him what she wanted or if he already had a clue.

"So Kathleen worked out well for you?"

"Yes," she said, easing out of her shoes. "She's a sweetheart and so efficient. She was able to find all the fabric I need and the cost of shipping won't be bad. I really hadn't expected you to set up the office like that. Thanks again for the roses. They were beautiful."

"You thanked me already for the flowers, and I'm glad you liked them. I plan to take you to the movies this weekend, but how would you like to watch a DVD now?"

She studied his features as he walked into the living room. Was that what he really wanted to do? "A movie on DVD sounds fine."

"You got a favorite?"

She chuckled as she dropped down on the sofa. "And if I do, should I just assume you have it here?"

He sat in the wingback chair across from her. "No, but I'm sure it can be ordered through my cable company. As I said, whatever you want, I will make it happen."

In that case. She stood from the sofa and in bare feet she slowly crossed the room and came to a stop between his opened legs. "Make love to me, Callum."

Callum didn't hesitate to pull Gemma down into his lap. He had been thinking about making love to her all day. That kiss in her office had whet his appetite and now he was about to be appeased. But first he had to tell her something before he forgot.

"Mom called. She's invited you to have lunch and go shopping with her, my sister and my sisters-in-law next Friday."

Surprise shone on Gemma's face. She twisted around in his arms to look up at him. "She did?"

"Yes."

"But why? I'm here to decorate your house. Why would they want to spend time with me?"

Callum chuckled. "Why wouldn't they? You've never been to Australia and I gather from the conversations the other day they figured you like to shop like most other women."

"The same way men like watching sports. I understand that sports are just as popular here in this country as in the States."

"Yes, I played Australian rules football a lot growing up. Not sure how my body would handle it now, though," he said, adjusting her in his lap to place the top of his chin on the crown of her head. "I also like playing cricket. One day I'm going to teach you how to play."

"Well, you must have plans to do that during the time I'm here, because once I return home it's back to tennis for me."

Callum knew Gemma played tennis and that she was good at it. But what stuck out more than anything was her mentioning returning home. He didn't intend for that to happen, at least not on a permanent basis. "How can you think of returning to Denver when you still have so much to do here?"

She smiled. "Hey, give me a break. Today was my first full day on the job. Besides, you hired Kathleen for me. She placed all the orders and I even hired the company to come in and hang the drapes and pictures. Everything is moving smoothly. Piece of cake. I'll have that place decorated and be out of here in no time."

He didn't say anything for a moment, thinking he definitely didn't like the sound of that. Then he turned her in his arms. "I think we got sidetracked."

She looked up at him. "Did we?"

"Yes. You wanted to make love."

She tilted her head. "Umm, did I?"

"Yes."

She shook her head, trying to hide a grin, which he saw anyway. "Sorry, your time is up."

He stood with her in his arms. "I don't think so."

Callum carried her over to the sofa and sat down with her in his arms. "We have more room here," he said, adjusting her body in his lap to face him. "Now tell me what you want again."

"I don't remember," she said, amusement shining in her gaze.

"Sounds like you need another reminder," he said, standing.

She wrapped her arms around his neck. "Now where are you taking me?"

"To the kitchen. I think I'd like you for dessert."

"What! You're kidding, aren't you?"

"No. Watch me."

And she did. Gemma sat on the kitchen counter, where he placed her, while he rummaged through his refrigerator looking for God knows what. But she didn't mind, since she was getting a real nice view of his backside.

"Don't go anywhere. I'll have everything I need in a sec," he called out, still bent over, scouring his fridge.

"Oh, don't worry, I'm not going anywhere. I'm

enjoying the view," she said, smiling, her gaze still glued to his taut tush.

"The view is nice this time of night, isn't it?" he asked over his shoulder.

She grinned as she studied how the denim of his jeans stretched over his butt. He thought she was talking about the view of the ocean outside the window. "I think this particular view is nice anytime. Day or night."

"You're probably right."

"I know I am," Gemma said, fighting to keep the smile out of her voice.

Moments later Callum turned away from the refrigerator and closed the door with his hands full of items. He glanced over at Gemma. She was smiling. He arched a brow. "What's so funny?"

"Nothing. What you got there?"

"See for yourself," he said, placing all the items on the counter next to her.

She picked up a jar. "Cherries?"

A slow smile touched his lips at the same time she saw a hint of heat fill his green eyes. "My favorite fruit."

"Yeah, I'll bet."

She picked up another item. "Whipped cream?"

"For the topping."

She shook her head as she placed the whipped cream back on the counter and selected another item. "Nuts?"

"They go well with cherries," he said, laughing.

"You're awful."

"No, I'm not.

She picked up the final item. "Chocolate syrup?"

"That's a must," he said, rolling up his sleeve.

Gemma watched as he began taking the tops off all the containers. "So what are you going to do with all that stuff?"

He smiled. "You'll see. I told you that you're going to be my dessert."

She blinked when she read his thoughts. He was serious.

"Now for my fantasy," he said, turning to her and placing his hands on her knees as he stepped between them, widening her legs as he did so. He began unbuttoning her shirt and when he took it off her shoulders he neatly placed it on the back of the kitchen chair.

He reached out to unsnap the front of her bra, lifting a brow at its peach color. He'd watched her put it on this morning and when he asked her about it, she told him she liked matching undies.

"Nice color."

"Glad you like it."

Gemma couldn't believe it a short while later when she was sitting on Callum's kitchen counter in nothing but her panties. He then slid her into his arms. "Where are we going now?"

"Out on the patio."

"More room?"

"Yes, more room, and the temperature tonight is unusually warm."

He carried her through the French doors to place her on the chaise longue. "I'll be back."

"Okay." Anticipation was flowing through her veins and she could feel her heart thudding in her chest. She'd never considered herself a sexual being, but Callum was proving just how passionate she could be. At least with him. She had a pretty good idea just what he planned to do and the thought was inciting every cell in her body to simmer with desire. The thought that couples did stuff like this behind closed doors, actually had fun being together, being adventurous while making love, had her wondering what she'd been missing all these years.

But she knew she hadn't been missing anything because the men she'd dated in the past hadn't been Callum. Besides being drop-dead gorgeous, the man certainly had a way with women. At least he had a way with her. He had made her first time memorable; not only in giving her pleasure but in the way he had taken care of her afterwards.

And then there were the flowers he'd sent today. And then at dinner, she had enjoyed their conversation where not only had he shared how his day had gone, but had given her a lot of interesting information about his homeland. This weekend he had offered to take her sailing on his father's yacht. She was looking forward to that.

While sitting across from him during dinner, every little thing had boosted up her desire for him. She couldn't wait to return here to be alone with him. It could be the way he would smile at her over the rim of his wineglass, or the way he would reach across the table and touch her hand on occasion for no reason at all. They had ordered different entrées and he had hand-fed her some of his when she was curious as to how his meal tasted.

Callum returned and she watched as he placed all the items on the small table beside her. The patio was dark, except for the light coming in from the kitchen and the moonlight overhead. They had eaten breakfast on the patio this morning and she knew there wasn't a single building on either side of them, just the ocean.

He pulled a small stool over to where she lay on her back, staring up at him. "When will you be my dessert?" she tried asking in a calm voice, but found that to be difficult when she felt her stomach churning.

"Whenever you want. Just ask. I'll give you whatever you want."

He'd been telling her that so much that she was beginning to believe it. "The ocean sounds so peaceful and relaxing. You'd better hope I don't fall asleep," she warned.

"If you do, I'll wake you."

She looked up at him, met his gaze and felt his heat. She'd told him last night there were no limitations. There still weren't. It had taken her twenty-four years to get to this point and she intended to enjoy it for all it was worth. Callum was making this a wonderful experience for her and she appreciated him for being fascinating as well as creative.

He moved off the stool just long enough to lean over her to remove her panties. "Nice pair," he said, while easing the silky material down her thighs and legs.

"Glad you like them."

"I like them off you even better," he said, balling them up and standing to put them into the back pocket of his jeans. "Now for my dessert."

"Enjoy yourself."

"I will, sweetheart."

It seemed that her entire body responded to his use of that endearment. He meant nothing by it—she was certain of it. But still, she couldn't help how rapidly her heart was beating from hearing it and how her stomach was fluttering in response to it.

While she lay there, she watched as Callum removed his shirt and tossed it aside before returning to his stool. He leaned close and she was tempted to reach out and run her fingertips across his naked chest, but then decided she wouldn't do that. This was his fantasy. He'd fulfilled hers last night.

"Now for something sweet, like you," he said, and she nearly jumped when she felt a warm, thick substance being smeared over her chest with his fingers and hands in a sensual and erotic pattern. When he moved to her stomach the muscles tightened as he continued rubbing the substance all over her belly, as if he was painting a design on her.

"What is it?"

"My name."

His voice was husky and in the moonlight she saw his tense features, the darkness of the eyes staring back at her, the sexy line of his mouth. All she could do was lie there and stare up at him speechlessly, trying to make sense of what he said. He was placing his name on her stomach as if he was branding her as his. She forced the thought from her mind, knowing he didn't mean anything by it.

"How does it feel?" he asked as his hand continued spreading chocolate syrup all over her.

"The chocolate feels sticky, but your hands feel good," she said honestly. He had moved his hands down past her stomach to her thighs.

He didn't say anything for a long moment, just continued to do what he was doing.

"And this is your fantasy?" she asked.

His lips curved into a slow smile that seemed to heat his gaze even more. "Yes. You'll see why in a moment."

When Callum was satisfied that he had smeared enough chocolate syrup over Gemma's body, he grabbed the can of whipped cream and squirted some around her nipples, outlined her belly button, completely covered her feminine mound, and made squiggly lines on her thighs and legs.

"Now for the cherries and nuts," he said, still holding her gaze.

He then proceeded to sprinkle her with nuts and place cherries on top of the whipped cream on her breasts, navel and womanly mound. In fact, he placed several on the latter.

"You look beautiful," he said, taking a step back and looking down at her to see just what he'd done.

"I'll take your word for it," she said, feeling like a huge ice-cream sundae. "I just hope there isn't a colony of ants around."

He laughed. "There isn't. Now to get it off you."

She knew just how he intended to do that, but nothing prepared her for the feel of his tongue when he began slowly licking her all over. Every so often he would lean up and kiss her, giving her a taste of the concoction that was smeared all around his mouth, mingling his tongue with hers. At one point he carried a cherry with his teeth, placed it in her mouth and together they shared the taste.

"Callum…"

Callum loved the sound of his name on her lips and as he lowered his mouth back down to her chest, he could feel the softness of her breasts beneath his mouth. And each nipple tasted like a delicious pebble wrapped around his tongue. Every time he took one into his mouth she shivered, and he savored the sensation of sucking on them.

He kissed his way down her stomach and when he came to the area between her legs, he looked up at her, met her gaze and whispered, "Now I will devour you."

"Oh, Callum."

He dropped to his knees in front of her and homed in to taste her intimately. She cried out his name the moment his tongue touched her and she grabbed hold of his hair to hold his mouth hostage. There was no need, since he didn't plan to go anyplace until he'd licked his fill. Every time his tongue stroked her clitoris, her body would tremble beneath his mouth.

She began mumbling words he was certain had no meaning, but hearing her speak incoherently told him her state of mind. It was tortured, like his. She was the only woman he desired. The only woman he loved.

Moments later when she bucked beneath his mouth when her body was ripped by a massive sensual explosion, he kept his tongue planted deep inside her, determined to give her all the pleasure she deserved. All the pleasure she wanted.

When the aftershocks of her orgasm had passed, he pulled away and began removing his jeans. And then he moved his body in position over hers, sliding between her open legs and entering her in one smooth thrust.

He was home. And he began moving, stroking parts of her insides that his tongue hadn't been able to reach, but his manhood could. And this way he could connect with all of her now. This way. Mating with her while breathing in her delicious scent, as the taste of her was still embedded in his mouth.

The magnitude of what they were sharing sent him reeling over the top, and he felt his own body beginning to explode. He felt his release shoot straight into her the moment he called out her name.

Instinctively, her body began milking him again, pulling everything out of him, making him moan in pleasure. And he knew this was just a part of what he felt for her. And it wasn't lust. It was everything love was based on—the physical and the emotional. And he hoped she would see it. Every day she was here he would show her both sides of love. He would share his body with her. He would share his soul. And he would continue to make her his.

He was tempted to tell her right then and there how he felt, let her know she was his soul mate, but he knew he couldn't. Not yet. She had to realize for herself that there was more between them than this. She had to realize and believe that she was the only woman for him.

He believed that would happen and, thankfully, he had a little time on his side to break down her defenses, to get her to see that all men weren't alike, and that he was the man destined to love her forever.

"So what do you think of this one, Gemma?" Mira Austell asked, showing Gemma the diamond earrings dangling from her ears.

"They're beautiful," Gemma said, and truly meant it.

The Austell ladies had picked her up around ten and it was almost four in the afternoon and they were still at it. Gemma didn't want to think about all the stores they had patronized or how many bags they had between the five of them.

Gemma had seen this gorgeous pair of sandals she just had to buy and also a party dress, since Callum had offered to take her to a club on the beach when she mentioned that she enjoyed dancing.

This particular place—an upscale jewelry store—was their last stop before calling it a day. Le'Claire suggested they stop here, since she wanted a new pair of pearl earrings.

"Gemma, Mira, come look at all these gorgeous rings," Le'Shaunda was saying, and within seconds they were all crowded around the glass case.

"I really like that one," Annette said, picking out a solitaire with a large stone.

"Umm, and I like that one," Le'Claire said, smiling. "I have a birthday coming up soon, so it's time to start dropping hints."

Gemma thought Callum's mother was beautiful and could understand how his father had fallen in love so fast. And no wonder Todd gave her anything she wanted. But then Callum gave her anything she wanted as well. Like father, like son. Todd had trained his offspring well. Last weekend Callum had treated her to a picnic on the beach, and another one was planned for this weekend as well. She had enjoyed her time with him and couldn't help but appreciate the time and attention he gave to her when he really didn't have to do so.

"Gemma, which of these do you like the best?" Le'Claire asked.

Gemma pressed her nose to the glass case as she peered inside. All the rings were beautiful and no doubt expensive. But if she had to choose…

"That one," she said, pointing to a gorgeous four-carat, white-gold, emerald-cut ring. "I think that's simply beautiful."

The other ladies agreed, and each picked out their favorites. The store clerk even let everyone try them on to see how each ring looked on their hands. Gemma was amused by how the others said they would remind their husbands about those favorites when it got close to their birthdays.

"It's almost dinnertime, so we might as well go somewhere to get something to eat," Le'Shaunda said. "I know a wonderful restaurant nearby."

Le'Claire beamed. "That's a wonderful idea."

Gemma thought it was a wonderful idea as well, although she missed seeing Callum. He had begun joining her for lunch every day at her office, always bringing good sandwiches for her to eat and wine to drink. They usually went out to a restaurant in town for dinner. Tonight they planned to watch a movie and make love. Or they would make love and then watch a movie. She liked the latter better, since they could make love again after the movie.

"Did Callum mention anything to you about a hunting trip in a couple of weeks?" Annette asked.

Gemma smiled over at her. "Yes, he did. I understand all the men are leaving for a six-day trip."

"Yes," Mira said as if she was eager for Colin to be

gone. The other woman glanced over at Gemma and explained. "Of course I'm going to miss my husband, but that's when we ladies get to do another shopping trip."

Everyone laughed and Gemma couldn't keep from laughing right along with them.

Thirteen

"Hello," Gemma mumbled into the telephone receiver.

"Wake up, sleepy."

A smile touched Gemma's lips as she slowly forced her eyes fully open. "Callum," she whispered.

"Who else?"

She smiled sleepily. He had left two days ago on a hunting trip with his father and brothers and would be gone for another four days. "I've been thinking about you."

"I've been thinking about you, too, sweetheart. I miss you already," he said.

"And I miss you, too," she said, realizing at that moment just how much. He had taken her to a party at his friend's home last weekend and she had felt special walking in with him. And he'd never left her side. It was nice meeting some of the guys he'd gone to college with. And the night before leaving to go hunting he'd taken her to the movies again. He filled a lot of her time when she wasn't working, so yes, she did miss him already.

"That's good to hear. You had a busy day yesterday, right?"

She pulled herself up in bed. "Yes, but Kathleen and I were able to make sure everything would be delivered as planned."

"Don't forget, you promised to take a break and let me fly you to India when I get back."

"Yes, and I'm looking forward to it, although I hope there isn't a lot of turbulence on that flight."

"You never know, but you'll be with me and I'll take care of you."

Her smile widened. "You always do."

A few moments later they ended the call, and she fluffed her pillow and stretched out in the bed. It was hard to believe that she had been in Australia four weeks already. Four glorious weeks. She missed her family and friends back home, but Callum and his family were wonderful and treated her like she was one of them.

She planned to go shopping with his mother, sister and sisters-in-law again tomorrow, and then there would be a sleepover at Le'Claire's home. She genuinely liked the Austell women and had had some rather amusing moments when they'd shared just how they handled their men. It had been hilarious when Le'Claire even gave pointers to Le'Shaunda, who claimed her husband could be stubborn at times.

But nothing, Gemma thought, could top all the times she'd spent with Callum. They could discuss anything.

When she'd received the call that Niecee had been arrested, she had let him handle it so that her emotions wouldn't stop her from making sure the woman was punished for what she had done. And then there were the flowers he continued to send her every week, and the "I'm thinking of you" notes that he would leave around the house for her to find. She stared up at the ceiling, thinking that Callum was definitely not like other men. The woman he married would be very lucky.

At that moment a sharp pain settled around her heart at the thought of any other woman with Callum, sharing anything close to what they had shared this past month. To know that another woman, his soul mate, would be living with him in the house she was decorating almost made her ill.

She eased to the edge of the bed, knowing why she felt that way. She had fallen in love with him. "Oh, no!"

She dropped back on the bed and covered her face with her hands. How did she let that happen? Although Callum wouldn't intentionally break her heart, he would break it just the same. How could she have fallen in love with him? She knew the answer without much thought. Callum was an easy man to love. But it wasn't meant for her to be the one to love him. He had told her about his soul mate.

She got out of bed and headed for the bathroom, knowing what she had to do. There was no way she would not finish the job she came here to do, but she needed to return home for at least a week or two to get her head screwed back on straight. Kathleen could handle things until she returned. And when she got back, she'd be capable of handling a relationship with Callum the way it should be handled. She would still love him, but at least she would have thought things through and come to the realization she couldn't ever be the number one woman in his life. She'd have to be satisfied with that.

A few hours later she had showered, dressed and packed a few of her things. She had called Kathleen and given her instructions as to what needed to be done in her absence, and assured the older woman that she would be back in a week or so.

Gemma decided not to call Callum to tell him she was leaving. He would wonder why she was taking off all of a sudden. She would think of an excuse to give him when she got home to Denver. She wiped the tears from her eyes. She had let the one thing happen to her that she'd always sworn would never happen.

She had fallen in love with a man who didn't love her.

Callum stood on the porch of the cabin and glanced all around. Nothing, he thought, was more beautiful than the Australian outback. He could recall the first time he'd come to this cabin as a child with his brothers, father and grandfather.

His thoughts drifted to Gemma. He knew for certain that she was his soul mate. The last month had been idyllic. Waking up with her in his arms every morning, making love with her each night, was as perfect as perfect could get. And he was waiting patiently for her to realize that she loved him, too.

It would be then that they would talk about it and he

would tell her that he loved her as well, that he'd known for a while that she was the one, but had wanted her to come to that realization on her own.

Callum took a sip of his coffee. He had a feeling she was beginning to realize it. More than once over the past week he'd caught her staring at him with an odd look on her face, as if she was trying to figure out something. And at night when she gave herself to him, it was as if he would forever be the only man in her life. Just as, when he made love to her, he wanted her to believe that she would forever be the only woman in his.

"Callum. You got a call. It's Mom."

Morris's voice intruded on his thoughts and he reentered the cabin and picked up the phone. "Yes, Mom?"

"Callum, it's Gemma."

His heart nearly stopped beating. He knew the ladies had a shopping trip planned for tomorrow. "What's wrong with Gemma? What happened?"

"I'm not sure. She called and asked me to take her to the airport."

"Airport?"

"Yes. She said she had to return home for a while, and I could tell she'd been crying."

He rubbed his forehead. That didn't make any sense. He'd just spoken to her that morning and she was fine. She had two pregnant sisters-in-law and he hoped nothing had happened. "Did she say why she was leaving, Mom? Did she mention anything about a family crisis?"

"No, in fact I asked and she said it had nothing to do with her family."

Callum pulled in a deep breath, not understanding any of this.

"Have you told her yet that you're in love with her, Callum?"

"No. I didn't want to rush her and was giving us time to develop a relationship before doing that. I wanted her to see from my actions that I loved her and get her to admit to herself that she loved me, too."

"Now I understand completely," Le'Claire said softly.

"You do?"

"Yes."

"Then how about explaining things to me because I'm confused."

He heard his mother's soft chuckle. "You're a man, so you would be. I think the reason Gemma left is because she realizes that she loves you. She's running away."

Callum was even more confused. "Why would she do something like that?"

"Because if she loves you and you don't love her back then—"

"But I do love her back."

"But she doesn't know that. And if you explained about waiting for a soul mate the way you explained it to me, she's probably thinking it's not her."

The moment his mother's words hit home, Callum threw his head back in frustration and groaned. "I think you're right, Mom."

"I think I'm right, too. So what are you going to do?"

A smile cascaded across Callum's lips. "I'm going after my woman."

Fourteen

Ramsey Westmoreland had been in the south pasture most of the day, but when he got home he'd heard from Chloe that Gemma was back. She'd called for Megan to pick her up at the airport. And according to what Megan had shared with Chloe, Gemma looked like she'd cried during the entire eighteen-hour flight.

He was about to place a call to Callum to find out what the hell had happened when he received a call from Colin saying Callum was on his way to Denver. The last thing Ramsey needed in his life was drama. He'd had more than enough during his affair with Chloe.

But here he was getting out of his truck to go knock on the door to make sure Gemma was all right. Callum was on his way and Ramsey would leave it to his best friend to handle Gemma from here on out because his sister could definitely be Miss Drama Queen. And seeing that she was here at Callum's cabin and not at her own place spoke volumes, whether she knew it or not. However, for now he would play the dumb-ass, just to satisfy his curiosity. And Chloe's.

He knocked on the door and it was yanked open. For a moment he was taken aback. Gemma looked like a mess, but he had enough sense not to tell her that. Instead, he took off his hat, passed by her and said in a calm tone. "Back from Australia early, aren't you?"

"Just here for a week or two. I'm going back," she said in a strained voice, which he pretended not to hear.

"Where's Callum? I'm surprised he let you come by yourself, knowing how afraid you are of flying. Was there a lot of turbulence?"

"I didn't notice."

Probably because you were too busy crying your eyes out. He hadn't seen her look like this since their parents' funeral. Ramsey leaned against a table in the living room and glanced around. He then looked back at her. "Any reason you're here and not at your own place, Gemma?"

He knew it was the wrong question to ask when suddenly her mouth quivered and she started to sob. "I love him, but he doesn't love me. I'm not his soul mate. But that's okay. I can deal with it. I just didn't want to ever cry over a man the way those girls used to do when Zane and Derringer broke up with them. I swore that would *never* happen to me. I swore I would never be one of them and fall for a guy who didn't love me back."

Ramsey could only stare at her. She actually thought Callum didn't love her? He opened his mouth to tell her just how wrong she was, then suddenly closed it. It was not his place to tell her anything. He would gladly let Callum deal with this.

"Sorry, Ram, but I need to be alone for a minute." He then watched as she quickly walked into the bedroom and closed the door behind her.

Moments later Ramsey was outside, about to open the door to his truck to leave when a vehicle pulled up. He sighed in relief when he saw Callum quickly getting out of the car.

"Ramsey, I went to Gemma's place straight from the airport and she wasn't there. Where the hell is she?"

Ramsey leaned against his truck. Callum looked like he hadn't slept for a while. "She's inside and I'm out of here. I'll let you deal with it."

Callum paused before entering his cabin. Ramsey had jumped into his truck and left in a hurry. Had Gemma trashed his place or something? Drawing in a deep breath, he removed his hat before slowly opening the door.

He strolled into the living room and glanced around. Everything was in order, but Gemma was nowhere in sight. Then he heard a sound coming from the bedroom. He perked up his ears. It was Gemma and she was crying. The sound tore at his heart.

Placing his hat on the rack, he quickly crossed the room and opened his bedroom door. And there she was, lying in his bed with her head buried in his pillows.

He quietly closed the door behind him and leaned against it. Although he loved her and she loved him, he was still responsible for breaking her heart. But, if nothing else, he'd learned over the past four weeks that the only way to handle Gemma was to let her think she was in control, even when she really wasn't. And even if you had to piss her off a little in the process.

"Gemma?"

She jerked up so fast he thought she was going to tumble out of the bed. "Callum! What are you doing here?" She stood quickly, but not before giving one last swipe to her eyes.

"I could ask you the same thing, since this is my place," he said, crossing his arms over his chest.

She threw her hair over her shoulder. "I knew you weren't here," she said as if that explained everything. It didn't.

"So you took off from Australia, left a job unfinished, got on a plane although you hate flying to come here. For what reason, Gemma?"

She lifted her chin and glared at him. "I don't have to answer that, since it's none of your business."

Callum couldn't help but smile at that. He moved away from the door to stand in front of her. "Wrong. It is my business. Both business and personal. It's business because I hired you to do a job and you're not there doing it. And it's personal because it's you and anything involving you is personal to me."

She lifted her chin a little higher. "I don't know why."

"Well, then, Gemma Westmoreland, let me explain it to you," he said, leaning in close to her face. "It's personal because you mean everything to me."

"I can't and I don't," she snapped. "Go tell that to the woman you're going to marry. The woman who is your soul mate."

"I am telling that to her. You are her."

She narrowed her eyes. "No, I'm not."

"Yes, you are. Why do you think I hung around here for three years working my tail off? Not because I needed the job, but because the woman I love, the woman who's had my heart since the first day I saw her, was here. The woman I knew the moment I saw her that she was destined to be mine. Do you know how many nights I went to this bed thinking of you, dreaming of you, patiently waiting for the day when I could make you belong to me in every possible way?"

He didn't give her a chance to answer him. Figured she probably couldn't anyway with the shocked look on her face, so he continued. "I took you to Australia for two reasons. First, I knew you could do the job, and secondly, I wanted you on my turf so I could court you properly. I wanted to show you that I was a guy worth your love and trust. I wanted you to believe in me, believe that I would never break your heart because, no matter what you thought, I was always going to be there for you. To give you every single thing you wanted. I love you."

There, he had his say and he knew it was time to brace himself when she had hers. She shook her head as if to mentally clear her mind and then she glanced back up at him. And glared.

"Are you saying that I'm the reason you hung around here and worked for Ramsey and that you took me to Australia to decorate your house and to win me over?"

She had explained it differently, but it all came down to the same thing. "Yes, that about sums it all up, but don't forget the part about loving you."

She threw her hands up in the air and then began angrily pacing the room while saying, "You put me through all this for nothing! You had me thinking I was decorating that house for another woman. You had me thinking that we were just having an affair that would lead nowhere."

She stopped pacing and her frown deepened. "Why didn't you tell me the truth?"

He crossed the room to stand in front of her. "Had I told you the truth, sweetheart, you would not have been ready to hear it, nor would you have believed it. You would have given me more grief than either of us needed," he said softly.

A smile then crossed his lips. "I had threatened to kidnap you, but Ramsey thought that was going a little too far."

Her eyes widened. "Ramsey knew?"

"Of course. Your brother is a smart man. There's no way I could have hung around here for three years sniffing around his sister and he not know about it."

"Sniffing around me? I want you to know that I—"

He thought she'd talked enough and decided to shut her up by pulling her into his arms and taking her mouth. The moment his tongue slid between her lips he figured she would either bite it or accept it. She accepted it and it began tangling with hers.

Callum deepened the kiss and tightened his hold on Gemma and she responded by wrapping her arms around his neck, standing on tiptoes and participating in their kiss the way he'd shown her how to do. He knew they still had a lot to talk about, and he would have to go over it again to satisfy her, but he didn't care. He would always give her what she wanted.

Callum forced his mouth from hers, but not before taking a quick lick around her lips. He then rested his forehead against hers and pulled in a deep breath. "I love you, Gemma," he whispered against her temple. "I loved you from the moment I first saw you. I knew you were the one, my true soul mate."

Gemma dropped her head to Callum's chest and wrapped her arms around his waist, breathing in his scent and glowing in his love. She was still reeling from his profession of love for her. Her heart was bursting with happiness.

"Gemma, will you marry me?"

She snatched her head up to look into his eyes. And there she saw in their green depths what she hadn't seen before. Now she did.

"Yes, I'll marry you, but…"

Callum chuckled. "There's a but?"

"Yes. I want to be told every day that you love me."

He rolled his eyes. "You've hung around my mom, sister and sisters-in-law too much."

"Whatever."

"I don't have a problem doing that. No problem at all." He sat down on the bed and pulled her down into his lap. "You never answered my question. What are you doing here and not at your place?"

She lowered her head, began toying with the buttons on his shirt and then glanced up and met his gaze. "I know it sounds crazy, but I came home to get over you, but once I got here I had to come here to feel close to you. I was going to sleep in this bed tonight because I knew this is where you slept."

Callum tightened his arms around her. "I got news for you, Gemma. You're *still* sleeping in this bed tonight. With me."

He eased back on the bed and took her with him, covering her mouth with his, kissing her in a way that let her know how much love he had for her. He adjusted their bodies so he could remove every stitch of her clothing and then proceeded to undress himself.

He returned to the bed and pulled her into his arms, but not before taking a small box from the pocket of his jacket. He placed his knee on the bed and pulled her into his arms to slide a ring on her finger. "For the woman who took my breath away the moment I saw her. To the woman I love."

Tears clouded Gemma's eyes when she gazed down at the beautiful ring Callum had placed on her finger. Her breath nearly stopped. She remembered the ring. She had seen it that day when she'd gone shopping with the Austell women and they had stopped by that jewelry store. Gemma had mentioned to Le'Claire how much she'd liked this particular one.

"Oh, Callum. Even your mom knows?" She had to fight back tears as she continued to admire her ring.

"Sweetheart, everybody knows," he said, grinning. "I had sworn them to secrecy. It was important for me to court you the way you deserved. You hadn't dated a whole lot, and I wanted to show you that not all guys were heartbreakers."

She wrapped her arms around his neck. "And you did court me. I just didn't know that's what you were doing. I just figured you were being nice, sending me those flowers, taking me to the movies and those picnic lunches on the beach. I just thought you were showing me how much you appreciated me…"

"In bed?"

"Yes."

"And that's what I was afraid of," he said, pulling her closer to him. "I didn't want you to think it was all about sex, because it wasn't. When I told you I would give you anything and everything you wanted, Gemma, I meant it. All you had to do was ask for it, even my love, which is something you already had."

She rested her head on his bare chest for a moment and then she lifted her head to look back at him. "Do you think you wasted three years living here, Callum?"

He shook his head. "No. Being here gave me a chance to love you from afar while watching you grow and mature into the beautiful woman you are today. I saw you gain your independence and then wear it like a brand of accomplishment in everything you did. I was so proud of you when you landed that big contract with the city, because I knew exactly what you could do. That gave me the idea to buy that house for you to decorate. That will be our home and the condo will become our private retreat when we want to spend time at the beach."

He paused a moment. "I know you'll miss your family and all, and—"

Gemma reached up and placed a finger to his lips. "Yes, I will miss my family, but my home will be with you. We will come back and visit and that will be good enough for me. I want to be in Sydney with you."

Callum didn't say anything for a moment and then asked. "What about your business here?"

Gemma smiled. "I'm closing it. I've already opened another shop in Sydney, thanks to you. Same name but different location."

Her smile widened. "I love you, Callum. I want to be your wife and have your babies and I promise to always make you happy."

"Oh, Gemma." He reached out and cupped her face with both hands, lightly brushing his lips against hers before taking it in a hard kiss, swallowing her breath in the process.

He shifted to lie down on the bed and took her with him, placing her body on top of his while he continued to kiss her with a need that made every part of his body feel sensitive.

He tore his mouth away from hers to pull in a much-needed breath, but she fisted her hands in his hair to bring his face closer, before nibbling on his lips and licking around the corners of his mouth. And when he released a deep moan, she slid her tongue into his mouth and begin kissing him the way she'd gotten used to him kissing her.

Callum felt his control slipping and knew this kiss would be imprinted on his brain forever. He deepened the kiss, felt his engorged sex press against the apex of her thighs, knowing just what it wanted. Just what it needed.

Just what it was going to get.

He pulled his mouth away long enough to adjust her body over his. While staring into her eyes, he pushed upward and thrust into her, immediately feeling her heat as he buried himself deep in her warmth. He pulled out and thrust in again while the hard nipples of her breasts grazed his chest.

And then she began riding him, moving her body on top of his in a way that had him catching his breath after every stroke. Together, they rode, they gave and took, mated in a way that touched everything inside of him; had him chanting her name over and over.

Then everything seemed to explode and he felt her body when it detonated. He soon followed, but continued hammering home, getting all he could and making her come again.

"Callum!"

"That's it, my love, feel the pleasure. Feel our love."

And then he leaned up and kissed her, took her mouth with a hunger that should already have been appeased. But he knew he would always want this. He would always want her, and he intended to never let her regret the day she'd given him her heart.

Totally sated, Gemma slowly opened her eyes and, like so many other times over the past weeks, Callum was in bed with her, and she was wrapped in his embrace. She snuggled closer and turned in his arms to find him watching her with satisfied passion in the depth of his green eyes.

She smiled at him. "I think we broke the bed."

He returned her smile and tightened his arms around her. "Probably did. But it can be fixed."

"If not, we can stay at my place," she offered.

"That will work."

At that moment the phone rang and he shifted their

bodies to reach and pick it up. "That's probably Mom, calling to make sure things between us are all right."

He picked up the phone. "Hello."

He nodded a few times. "Okay, we're on our way."

He glanced over at Gemma and smiled. "That was Dillon. Chloe's water broke and Ramsey rushed her to the hospital. Looks like there's going to be a new Westmoreland born tonight."

It didn't take long for Callum and Gemma to get to the hospital, and already it was crowded with Westmorelands. It was almost 3:00 a.m. If anyone was curious as to why they were all together at that time of the morning, no one mentioned it.

"The baby is already here," Bailey said, excited. "We have a girl, just like we wanted."

Callum couldn't help throwing his head back and laughing. Good old Ram had a daughter.

"How's Chloe?" Gemma asked.

"Ramsey came out a few moments ago and said she's fine," Megan said. "The baby is a surprise."

"Yes, we didn't expect her for another week," Dillon said grinning. He glanced over at his pregnant wife, Pam, and smiled as he pulled her closer to him. "That makes me nervous."

"Has anyone called and told Chloe's father?"

"Yes," Chloe's best friend, Lucia, said smiling. "He's a happy grandpa and he'll be here sometime tomorrow."

"What's the baby's name?" Callum asked.

It was Derringer who spoke up. "They are naming her Susan after Mom. And they're using Chloe's mom's name as her middle name."

Gemma smiled. She knew Chloe had lost her mother at an early age, too. "Oh, that's nice. Our parents' first grand. They would be proud."

"They *are* proud," Dillon said, playfully tapping her nose.

"Hey, is this an engagement ring?" Bailey asked loudly, grabbing Gemma's hand.

Gemma glanced up at Callum and smiled lovingly. "Yes, we're getting married."

Cheers went up in the hospital waiting room. The Westmorelands had a lot to celebrate.

Zane glanced over at Dillon and Pam. "I guess now we're depending on you two to keep us male Westmorelands in the majority."

"Yeah," Derringer agreed.

"You know the two of you could find ladies to marry and start making your own babies," Megan said sweetly to her brothers. Her suggestion did exactly what she'd expected it to do—zip their lips.

Callum pulled Gemma closer into his arms. They shared a look. They didn't care if they had boys or girls—they just wanted babies. There were not going to be any hassles getting a big family out of them.

"Happy?" Callum asked.

"Extremely," she whispered.

Callum looked forward to when they would be alone again and he bent and told her just what he intended to do when they got back to the cabin.

Gemma blushed. Megan shot her sister a look. "You okay, Gem?"

Gemma smiled, glanced up at Callum and then back at her sister. "Yes, I couldn't be better."

Epilogue

There is nothing like a Westmoreland wedding, and this one was extra special because guests came from as far away as Australia and the Middle East. Gemma glanced out at the single ladies, waiting to catch her bouquet. She turned her back to the crowd, closed her eyes and threw it high over her head.

When she heard all the cheering, she turned around and smiled. It had been caught by Lucia Conyers, Chloe's best friend. She glanced across the room and looked at the two new babies. As if Susan's birth had started a trend, Dillon and Pam's son, Denver, came early, too.

"When can we sneak away?"

"You've waited three years. Another three hours won't kill you," she jokingly replied to her husband of two hours.

"Don't be so sure about that," was his quick response.

Their bags were packed and he was going to take her to India, as they'd planned before. Then they would visit Korea and Japan. She wanted to get decorating ideas with a few Asian pieces.

Callum took his wife's hand in his as they moved around the ballroom. He had been introduced to all the Atlanta Westmorelands before when he was invited to the Westmoreland family reunion as a guest. Now he would attend the next one as a bona fide member of the Westmoreland clan.

"How soon do you want to start making a baby?"

Gemma almost choked on her punch. He gave her a few pats on the back and grinned. "Didn't mean for you to gag."

"Can we at least wait until we're alone?"

"To talk about it or to get things started?"

Gemma chuckled as she shook her head. "Why do I get the feeling there will never be a dull moment with you?"

He pulled her closer to him. "Because there won't be. Remember I'm the one who knows what a Westmoreland wants. At least I know what my Westmoreland wants."

Gemma wrapped her arms around his neck. "I'm an Austell now," she said proudly.

"Oh, yes, I know. And trust me—I will never let you forget it."

Callum then pulled her into his arms and in front of all their wedding guests, he kissed her with all the love flowing in his heart. He had in his arms everything he'd ever wanted.

* * * * *

Silhouette Desire

COMING NEXT MONTH
Available October 12, 2010

#2041 ULTIMATUM: MARRIAGE
Ann Major
Man of the Month

#2042 TAMING HER BILLIONAIRE BOSS
Maxine Sullivan
Dynasties: The Jarrods

#2043 CINDERELLA & THE CEO
Maureen Child
Kings of California

#2044 FOR THE SAKE OF THE SECRET CHILD
Yvonne Lindsay
Wed at Any Price

#2045 SAVED BY THE SHEIKH!
Tessa Radley

#2046 FROM BOARDROOM TO WEDDING BED?
Jules Bennett

REQUEST YOUR FREE BOOKS!

2 FREE NOVELS
PLUS 2
FREE GIFTS!

™ *Silhouette*®

Desire®

Passionate, Powerful, Provocative!

HARLEQUIN®

A Romance

FOR EVERY MOOD™

Spotlight on

Inspirational

Wholesome romances
that touch the heart and soul.

See the next page
to enjoy a sneak peek from
the Love Inspired® inspirational series.